Tere Bina Jiya Jaaye Na

Love: A Force of Destiny

Parthasarthi Daas

Become
Shakespeare
.com

First published in 2015 by

BecomeShakespeare.com
Wordit Content Design & Editing Services Pvt Ltd
Newbridge Business Centre, C38/39,
Parinee Crescenzo Building, G Block,
Bandra Kurla Complex, Bandra East,
Mumbai 400 051, India
T: +91 8080226699

ISBN 978-93-83952-53-3

This book is dedicated to my family and friends.

Together, they are an incredible source of inspiration, and I am grateful to have been gifted with such positive people around me.

Special thanks to my wife, Shaloo Daas, who has always been by my side.

Chapter 1

February 2015

The ambulance swiftly pushed through the streets of Kolkata and made its way into the hospital compound, the siren blaring and the red light blinking in urgency, making sure that everyone was out of its way. As the door to the service elevator opened, two ward boys and a supervising nurse rushed out with a stretcher in tow. The nurse resigned to her duty of ensuring that the white towel covering the patient's forehead was always moist.

On the stretcher lay Aahuti Banerjee, a beautiful 27-year-old woman in the final stages of her pregnancy. Accompanying her and holding her hands was her husband, Biplav Banerjee, a handsome man of 30, his features marred by creases of worry and concern for his wife.

With them were Aahuti's family members: Arijit Sengupta, her father, a really fat and squat man of 49; Dolly Sengupta, her 44-year-old mother; and Jyotirmoi, her young, 21-year-old brother. Biplav's family also made their way through: his *bhabhi*, Sudha Banerjee of 47 years of age, and Jhantu, a thin balding man in his late 30s.

Aahuti seemed to be delirious because of high fever, and kept repeating to Biplav, Sudha, and her parents, 'I swear to God, if my child is born with my disease, I will choke it and kill it." Biplav, Sudha, Arijit, and Dolly tried their best to stop Aahuti from thinking such things, and hoped for the best. They prayed to Kali Maa. The doctors soon rolled Aahuti into the operation theatre, leaving her family outside waiting for her.

As they took a breather, Dr. Balraj Chugani, a slim and practical man in his early 50s, joined them. They all turned to him, feeling slightly relieved by his presence, as Biplav told him that Aahuti's mild fever from earlier in the day shot up around 11 p.m., and her labour pains soon followed, which is why they had to rush her to the hospital. Dr. Chugani reassured him, telling him that he did the right thing, and that there was no need to panic and worry. All they could do now was wait and pray to God for her well-being.

While Sudha held on to Biplav's arm, reassuring him of her safety in the hands of the doctors, the light atop the doors of the operation theatre came to life, and snapped Biplav out of his stupor. As he stared continuously into the red light, he drifted back into the past, to his memories from several years ago.

Chapter 2

February 2014

Under the looming glare of the old red sandstone building of the Alipore Central Jail, the Superintendent walked around the prison courtyard, passing the inmates who bowed and saluted him respectfully. He made his way into a room where an accountancy class was being conducted for a bunch of convicts, with the accounts teacher being none other than Biplav Banerjee.

Then in his late 20s, Biplav wore a hardened look on his otherwise pleasant and handsome face, partially hidden under a thick stubble. The Superintendent interrupted the class to have a word with him. He informed Biplav and the other inmates that the authorities had accepted Biplav's request of getting a release from the jail one day prior to the fixed date, and that meant that he was free to go the very same day. He said to Biplav, "Congratulations, son. You are now a free man."

While he made his way out and left Biplav to his class, the Superintendent stopped and said, "Meet me in my office when you are ready to leave. Don't forget." Hearing this, Biplav's body language suddenly changed, and he appeared to be nervous and edgy as he bid an emotional farewell to his fellow inmates. As he left, he put a bright young fellow in glasses in charge of his class.

Outside, in the courtyard, he met a rough looking fellow prisoner, Mukhtar *Bhai*, and told him that he was getting an early release. As he informed him of this, he asked for the phone number that *Bhai* had promised him. Mukhtar asked for a pen and wrote a phone number on Biplav's hand. In response, Biplav said, "Thank you, Mukhtar *Bhai*," and waved goodbye.

While he shed his prison uniform for his civilian attire, his face grew increasingly determined, like that of a man whose mind was set on something. He went out and met the Superintendent in his office, where the Superintendent handed Biplav some money. He said, "Here's the total wage you earned during your time here. Good luck with your life, Biplav."

Thanking him, Biplav left the office and was then led through the exit gates. Soon, he found himself outside the jail premises. He hailed a taxi and hopped in. "*Mujhe* Sealdah *le chalo* (Take me to Sealdah)," he ordered the cabbie, and soon enough, he was on his way.

*****

47-year-old Dr. Bishwanath Banerjee and his wife Sudha Banerjee faced the Superintendent, as Bishwanath reprimanded him for his not having informed them that they had let out Biplav one day prior to his release date. The Superintendent defended himself, saying, "Because of Biplav's exemplary conduct during his one year incarceration, the authorities paid heed to his request to let him go a day before his release date, as he wanted to go home and meet *you*, rather than have you go through the trouble of coming here to take him. He filed an application, and the permission was given by the authorities the day before." He added, "Biplav, being an educated and intelligent man, gave me no reason to distrust him."

Bishwanath asked, "Does he have any money on him?" The Superintendent nodded in affirmation. "About 14,000 rupees," he said. Bishwanath was surprised—so much money! The Superintendent said, "Prisoners get paid for the work they do during their time at the prison when they leave. Almost all prisoners did manual labour, indulged in some craft, or worked at the printing press, but Biplav used to teach regularly at the school for the prisoners, and everybody used to respect him for his hard work and intelligence. After all, it was a rare thing for the prisoners to have a Chartered Accountant among them teaching them accountancy, and Biplav turned out to be a brilliant teacher." The Superintendent continued, "He even motivated a few of the prisoners to pursue a career in accountancy after they were to get out of here."

Hearing this, Sudha was unable to hold herself back and burst into tears, as the Superintendent's tale reminded her painfully of Biplav. Sobbing, she asked Bishwanath, "After all this, where did Biplav go, leaving us all alone?"

"In many cases," said the Superintendent, "I find that after their release, prisoners go and stay in a cheap motel for a day or two to get used to their freedom before going home. So Biplav may have done the same. If he doesn't come home in time, then I urge you to file a police report."

Meanwhile, in Sealdah, an SUV was making its way through the chaotic and crowded MG Road. Salil Acharya, 27 and bespectacled, dressed in corporate clothes, rolled down the glass window as he peered out, trying to locate a landmark. He spotted the Santiniketan Hotel board behind a cluster of local buses bound for Howrah, and his eyes lit up.

*****

Soon after his release, Biplav had managed to secure a room in a cheap motel in Sealdah. It was a small room with large windows on two sides. There was a single bed, a chair, a table, and wall mirror—it looked like a typical cheap guest house room. The noise from the street outside filled the room; the chaos of the heavy afternoon traffic, and an accompanying constant chorus of bus conductors yelling "Howrah, Howrah, Howrah..." at the top of their voices came pouring through. Salil, who had managed to locate Biplav, informed him of Saurabh and Koel's marriage, which took place four months ago. "It was a grand affair," Salil remarked.

He reminded Biplav that he did warn him about Saurabh as he opened his tiffin box. Biplav accepted his mistake and said, "I should never have trusted that bastard. Anyway, it would be better now to plan ahead rather than dwell on the mistakes of the past." Salil agreed and told him that he had to be back in office by 3 p.m. for an important meeting, so they ate lunch and discussed their plan of action.

The first thing Biplav needed from Salil was Rs. 20,000 to buy a pistol. It would cost about Rs. 30,000 and he had about Rs. 10,000 with him. He said to Salil, "I've made quite a few contacts in jail, and it won't be difficult for me to buy an unlicensed Chinese 9mm pistol." He showed him the phone number written on the palm of his hand, and added, "This number belongs to an illegal arms seller in Khidirpur."

Salil was scared and excited at the same time. "A real gun!" he exclaimed. "Yeah," Biplav assured him, "but with fake bullets, only to scare that bastard. If he fires the pistol in the air, close to his face, it will make a sound like that of a real bullet. Only then will he get scared and sign the confession I've drafted in the form of a notary on a Rs. 100 stamp paper which I got prepared only this morning."

Handing the paper over to Salil, he continued, "I want Saurabh Dalmiya to sign this paper, which will prove his guilt and my innocence. Only after that will I return to *dada* and *bhabhi*. I will need your help, Salil—not only with the money for buying the pistol, but also in executing the whole plan." He asked, "Will you help me?"

Salil chided him, "How can you ask me such questions?! And why didn't you tell me about the money over the phone? I could have easily brought the cash along." Biplav confessed that he had his doubts about whether he would come at all in the first place—after all, people change, even friends. "The CA association has cancelled my Certificate of Practice, so I'm not even sure when I will get a job and find a way to return your money," he said.

Salil grew sentimental. Softly, he remarked, "How could you even think that I would change colours when my friend is going through such a low phase? Anyway, put all that behind you and come along with me to a nearby ATM—I'll give you the money there." Indicating that they needed to leave early, they finished their meal quickly in order to carry out their plan.

*****

Later that evening, a thick bundle of money, about Rs. 30,000, was placed on the table, and an illegal gun seller was instructing them on how to handle a 9mm Chinese pistol, how to load bullets in it, how to remove the safety latch, how to fire it, etc. Finally, he handed the pistol to Biplav, who now went through the moves as the gun seller asked, "How is my cousin, Mukhtar *Bhai*? Has he been keeping well?" Biplav reassured him and told him that Mukhtar *Bhai* was doing great as he became comfortable with the pistol.

The gun seller asked him how many extra bullets he wanted with the pistol, as he gave only five cartridges free with the pistol. Biplav responded, "I don't want any real bullets. Do you have any fake bullets?" "Fake bullets?!" The gun seller retorted in astonishment, as the statement appeared to have hurt his ego. "I don't have anything fake for sale. If you want to buy fake bullets, you can go to a toyshop," he spat. "Mukhtar *Bhai* has started sending kids to buy guns from me now," he grumbled. Biplav paused for a minute to think, and finally decided that real bullets would do for him.

*****

The next morning, Bishwanath was seated comfortably by the window of his second storey house, reading his morning newspaper. A large two storey building that occupied a prominent space in the Old Ballygunj area of Kolkata, Bishwanath owned both floors, using the ground floor for his practice, Sudha Nursing Home. A big Gulmohar tree stood in the small house garden out in the front, covered in red flowers, and it dominated the view of the house. An ambulance was parked in the driveway, with Bishwanath's Ford car nearby, a large doctor's cross sticker on its windshield. Jhantu was busy cleaning the car in the driveway parking.

As he waited for his morning tea, he received a phone call from Biplav. Bishwanath called out to Sudha in the kitchen, who came into the living room with the tea tray. When Bishwanath informed her that it was Biplav on the line, she hurriedly put the tray on the table and grabbed the phone. She was desperate to know about his whereabouts and his well-being, and began to weep as she spoke to him.

Biplav, who was calling from a roadside PCO, calmly said to Sudha, "I am absolutely fine. I'll come back home in a day or two—I have some urgent work that I need to attend to first." After ending the phone call, Biplav wandered to a nearby tea stall and called for some tea.

*****

That night, Saurabh Dalmiya, a 27-year-old slightly plump and handsome rich Marwari, stood in front of the dressing table mirror in his bedroom, doing what he loved most—admiring himself. He was fresh out of the shower, was busy applying gel to his hair, getting ready to go out partying on a Saturday night. His clothes and accessories screamed opulence, and he brushed his hair as he hummed a *bhajan* tune.

The sound of the evening *aarti* being performed somewhere in the house was prominent in the background. He sprayed a ton of perfume all over himself, admired his reflection one last time, and stepped out into the huge living room. On one side was a large temple, where a lot of his family members—mother, father, elder brothers, *bhabhis*, nieces, cousins, and others—were engrossed in the *puja*. Also present was Koel, his wife, who was the same age as him.

Saurabh went and kneeled before his family God. His mother did his *aarti*, put a *tika* on his forehead, and blessed him. Then, she turned to Koel and said, "See him off till the door, *beta*. He is heading for an important meeting." Koel nodded and obediently accompanied him to the main door.

She was suspicious of his actual plans, as she sensed that he was stepping out for fun. "It seems strange that you're going to meet foreign business clients without any files or papers, or even your laptop," she wondered out loud.

Saurabh rubbished her comments, "You are becoming too suspicious, and it will affect the whole family very negatively." He added, "You should think positive thoughts only." He took the keys of one of his cars from his driver, got into the car, and drove away from his large and lavish bungalow.

*****

Hidden in the shadows of the hotel parking, Salil sat in his SUV, gulping down whiskey. As Saurabh drove in and parked his car, he saw Salil drinking. He stepped out of his car, locked it and got into Salil's vehicle.

He was angry at Salil for not being patient and waiting for him before opening the bottle all by himself. An irritated Salil taunted him, "Do you really expect me to get a bottle of Jack Daniels and then wait for you?!" He confessed his helplessness before the commands of uncle Jack. Brushing away his excuses, Saurabh ordered Salil to make him a drink. Salil snorted, "Help yourself to one." He proceeded to turn on the ignition, and pulled his vehicle out of the parking.

"What's the occasion today, dude?" asked Saurabh, as he made himself a drink, "I have asked you out for some fun over a dozen times in the last two years, but you always said you had given it all up because of your relationship with Krutika." Salil told him that he had broken up with Krutika. He added, "Now, I want to enjoy my freedom, like I did in the good old days."

The bottle of Jack Daniels now sat between them, almost half empty, as Salil drove through the dark streets of Kolkata. Saurabh was now getting impatient and asked about the girl they were supposed to be picking up for Rs. 12,000. Salil checked the time and said, "It's 10:50 p.m. She should be standing around the next left turn. She's quite punctual."

He took the turn and immediately spotted a girl in a *burqa* standing on the sidewalk. There she was—he got excited. "That *burqawali*," Saurabh thought aloud, surprised. "Yes," Salil said. "Nowadays, so many college girls are getting into this profession that the *burqa* is quite handy for them to protect their identity from anybody out there. She'll take off her *burqa* once she is with us," Salil guaranteed, as he brought the car to a stop near her. He asked Saurabh to drive, as he wants to go to the back seat with her. Saurabh put his foot down—"I want to go first. You have to let me." Salil gave in and let Saurabh go first.

Saurabh squeezed through to the back seat and opened the door. The girl came and sat next to him as Salil drove off. Soon, his vehicle found itself speeding on the wide roads, when Saurabh was shocked to find the girl holding a pistol to his belly. Then, she pulled the *burqa* off her face, and Biplav stepped out from behind the veil. "How do you like *me*?" Biplav grinned, mimicking a girl's voice. "You like me, don't you?" Saurabh was too stunned to speak—he just blinked and looked at Biplav, then at Salil, and then turned back to Biplav. Salil answered instead, "Oh, I like you so much, baby!" and burst out laughing.

The SUV soon came to a stop in the middle of the Ishwarchand Vidyasagar Setu, which was almost deserted at this late hour, with only a few odd vehicles passing by. Inside the SUV, Salil asked Saurabh to sign the confession right then, as the car was now standing still and not moving anymore. Biplav held the notary paper for Saurabh to sign. Saurabh was in a state of drunken panic, and kept making one excuse after another. He suddenly began to feel suffocated, and wanted to step out in the open to get some fresh air.

Keeping the pistol pointed at him, Biplav decided to let him out. Pleading and mumbling a lot of tosh, purely out of fear, Saurabh began to move back. Right then, Biplav threatened to really shoot him if he tried to escape.

Saurabh noticed that Biplav was perspiring, and his hand was shaky and sweaty. He realised that Biplav would never have the guts to pull the trigger. He suddenly turned around and ran away. Biplav yelled for him to stop, but Saurabh just sprinted away on his wobbly legs.

Biplav pulled the trigger. The bullet missed Saurabh by few feet and hit a girl on her Scooty who was going along her way in Biplav's direction from the opposite side. She crashed her bike into the railings, and fell down on the road, as the bullet had pierced her right below the left collarbone.

Biplav and Salil remained frozen for a moment, completely shell-shocked. In that moment, Saurabh also stopped and turned to look back at what happened before he escaped. "Did that pistol have real bullets?" asked Salil. Biplav nodded in affirmation. A frightened Salil grabbed Biplav's arm and asked him to flee. Biplav shook his arm free and walked up to the wounded and bleeding girl.

Her name was Aahuti Sengupta, a young girl of 25. When Biplav first spotted her, his breath caught in his throat, for she was a thing of beauty. Her Bengali features stood out with her big, soft eyes, luscious long hair and sharp features. She was lying on the road helplessly as she saw Biplav approaching her, with the pistol in one hand. "Why did you shoot me?" she asked, "I don't even know you!" Saying this, she finally fell unconscious.

Biplav threw his pistol into the river and called out to Salil, "Help me take this girl to the car. We need to have her looked at by a doctor." A protesting Salil joined him reluctantly. They lifted the girl and put her into the back seat. They realised they would in big trouble if they took her to any private or government hospital as it would become a police case. There would also be a lot of delay before anyone attended to her, and she'd lose a lot of blood during that time. What if she died because of all this? Even Salil would be sentenced as an accomplice—this thought scared the hell out of Salil. However, if they didn't take her to any doctor or hospital, she'd bleed to death in a few hours.

Biplav was genuinely concerned for her. Salil suggested taking her to Sudha Nursing Home, which belonged to his elder brother, who could operate on her himself and save her life. Biplav realised that it would indeed be the best option.

During this conversation, Biplav spotted her mobile phone in a little pouch hanging from her neck. He took it out and saw that it was switched off. He wondered whether to switch it on when Salil warned him to let it remain switched off. Biplav put the mobile in his pocket. Feeling damn lucky that no police patrol van had come their way so far, and no passerby had stopped on their way out of curiosity, Salil asked Biplav to hurry as they picked up the Scooty and helmet and put them into the vehicle before driving off.

*****

Soon after Biplav and Salil found their way to Bishwanath's clinic, Bishwanath was faced with a dilemma. He realised that if he operated on the girl without informing the police about it, his medical license could be cancelled if he was caught. It would also be ethically wrong to do so. Hearing this, Biplav broke down in front of Sudha and Bishwanath out of sheer desperation. He was repentant for what he did, but he refused to let this innocent girl die because of his foolishness. He implored, "*Dada*, please save her. Else I will take her to the police and surrender myself." Patting Biplav's head, Bishwanath said, "Calm down. I promise I'll try my best to save the girl. While I clean her wound and prepare for the operation, run to the blood bank and get the blood we need for her."

While Biplav headed to the blood bank, a very tense looking Bishwanath examined Aahuti's bullet wound and cleaned it, while a nurse handed him the instruments and other required material.

*****

Biplav, Salil, and Jhantu hurried to a government hospital blood bank, where they meet Dr. Matthew Golmes, who was in charge of the blood bank during the night shift. Jhantu knew him well. He said to him, "Bishu*da* sent us here to acquire blood. I believe he called you before we arrived?"

Dr. Golmes nodded in affirmation and said, "Yes. The nursing home called, asking for 1200ml of AB+ blood." While he mentioned this, he asked a staff member to fetch the blood. Just as Biplav was done signing the log book, the three pouches were handed over to Jhantu. Dr. Golmes made further entries in the log book as Biplav quickly took out the money from his wallet, and paid the required amount for the blood before hurriedly making an exit.

That night, as a masked Bishwanath began operating on Aahuti, a nurse set up a blood pouch in the drip. Bishwanath then began to take out the bullet fragments from her body and dropped them in a small tray.

*****

On their way back to the nursing home, a worried Salil asked, "What if this girl decides to file an FIR against us?" Biplav, as a way of reassuring Salil, said, "If that does happen, then I'll take complete responsibility for the shooting, and keep you out of this."

Salil then asked, "Biplav, why did you load the pistol with real bullets?" Biplav told him about how he bought the real bullets because he couldn't find fake ones. Shaking his head in disbelief, Salil said, "If I had known there were real bullets in the pistol, I would never have come along with you."

Agitated over the situation, Salil drove off after telling Biplav to call him if he needed him again for anything. Biplav walked inside the gate when he saw Sudha coming out with Jhantu from inside the nursing home. She wanted to check the girl's Scooty for any handbag which might have her ID. They moved over to one side, where the dented Scooty was parked.

Sudha and Biplav looked on as Jhantu took the key out from the ignition and unlocked the pillion seat to check the storage space under it. Inside, he found a handbag. Taking the bag, Sudha rummaged through it and found a voter ID card—Aahuti Sengupta. Her address was on there too.

Sudha asked Biplav and Jhantu to go and inform her family members, and gave the ID to Biplav. Biplav remembered something—he brought out Aahuti's mobile phone from his pocket, put it in the bag, and then put the bag back in the rear storage area.

*****

Aahuti's ID in tow, Biplav and Jhantu got out of Bishwanath's car, which came to a stop just outside the large gates of a sprawling Victorian mansion that stood two storeys tall. The name plate on the gate read "Sri Arijit Sengupta". They walked through the gates, across the garden in front of the house and come to the door. The house seemed to be at least 60-70 years old, and belonged to a class of houses known in Bengal as *Bari*. The side of the house facing the street was completely occupied by 5-6 shops.

The lights on the second floor shone through the windows. Biplav rang the doorbell. A woman in her early 50s, Dolly Sengupta, peeped out from the open window and asked, "Who are you?" Holding up Aahuti's ID in one hand, Biplav responded, asking, "Does Aahuti Sengupta live here?" When Dolly questioned his query, Biplav informed her that she had met with an accident.

Shocked at this news, Dolly asked him to wait. She called out to her husband upstairs, "Arijit! Turn off the TV and hurry down here now!" She rushed down the stairs and opened the door in a state of total panic. Breathless and panting, and instantly boring her eyes into the ID, she showered Biplav with a volley of questions: "Where is she? How did the accident happen? Is she badly hurt? Are there any fractures? Is she losing a lot of blood? Did her Scooty get hit by a bus? These damn Kolkata buses! Who are you, by the way? Are you Aahuti's friend? What's your name?"

By this time, her husband, Arijit Sengupta, joined her and attempted to calm her down. He was clearly used to her hysterical nature, and he himself seemed to have developed a calm persona. She rambled on, "We have been up worried sick about her. She's never come home this late without informing us, and her phone was switched off as well!" She paused to catch her breath and continued, "She always switches off her mobile phone while riding her Scooty, but it's been switched off for three hours, and we were just about to call the police to lodge a complaint, fearing something bad might have happened to her. Oh God, how true our fears came to be!" She lamented and broke down.

In an attempt to calm her down, Arijit accosted her in a low voice, "Be quiet, I'm telling you. Let this fellow speak at least so we can know how Aahuti is." In an instant, Dolly fell silent and turned to Biplav.

*****

Following the episode at the Sengupta household, Jhantu drove the car, with Biplav in the passenger seat. Arijit sat in the back with Dolly, speaking to Colonel Prasenjit Dutta on his mobile phone. He said to him, "The boy has assured us that she has suffered only minor injuries—a few cuts and bruises. You don't need to bother coming here, Colonel –"

Suddenly, he turned to his wife, irritated by her chattering away next to him. In a stern voice, he snapped, "Didn't I tell you to keep quiet?" Dolly held her tongue as Arijit nodded into the phone, and asked Biplav for the address. "Sudha Nursing Home, 47 Old Ballygunj," replied Biplav. Arijit repeated the address into the phone and disconnected the call. Turning to Dolly, he said, "Colonel *Saheb* is coming to see Aahuti too." "Good," she responded, "He cares a lot about her," and began chattering away to Biplav and Jhantu once again.

Arijit explained, "Colonel Prasenjit Dutta was in the army, but he has the heart of a poet. He's not just Aahuti's boss, but like a godfather to her. We had called him as we were worried about Aahuti not having returned home till so late in the night, and he had told us that she had left office by 10:30 p.m., which would mean that she should have reached home by 11:15 p.m. But it was already half past midnight, and so, on one hand we thought she was at Arsalan, enjoying a plate of *biryani* as always—you see, every time she is late, she stops for some *biryani* there, but she always calls me first to ask if I'd like a plate as well. As she hadn't called up, Dolly was doubtful about her whereabouts, but I didn't take her seriously. By this time, you came and rang our doorbell."

"It all happened because of that damn Scooty," Dolly cursed. "I've told her countless times to drive the car to work, but she refuses to listen; she likes her Scooty. To make matters worse, she leaves the car behind for her brother. My son, Jyotirmoi, works in a call centre at night and drives to work. He comes back at 3:00 a.m. He works only for his pocket money. During the day, he studies Law. He's a good student; he stood first in the Jadhavpur University Law entrance examination, and he joined law school just because I wanted him to become a great judge. He's a very nice boy, and he's very loving. Aahuti is also affectionate, but she is too wilful. She did not study Law, and went on to get her Master's degree in Social Welfare instead; following which she joined an NGO. She likes to help those in need. She has a kind heart, but she is now too worked up and hassled all the time –" She suddenly realised that she didn't know how Aahuti met with an accident, and concluded her rant to question Biplav about it.

He lied to her, saying, "Aahuti's Scooty skidded on some oil spilt on the road, and hit the divider. Luckily, my friend and I were nearby, and we took her to my elder brother's nursing home." Dolly was impressed to know that Biplav's elder brother was a doctor and had his own private nursing home.

Then, Arijit asked, "Why didn't you take Aahuti to a private or government hospital nearby, rather than going all the way to Ballygunj from scene of the accident?" Biplav hesitated for a moment, and then continued his lie, "Since her injuries were fairly minor, I figured it would be fine taking her to a nursing home rather than to a hospital."

Once they reached the nursing home, Biplav introduced Arijit and Dolly to Sudha and Bishwanath. Bishwanath informed Arijit that the operation was successful, and that Aahuti was no longer in danger. A shocked Arijit exclaimed, "Operation?!" Mirroring Arijit's disbelief, Dolly asked, "What kind of operation did she have? Was the accident so serious that she needed to be operated on?" Trying to protect his brother while still giving the truth to the worried parents, Bishwanath said, "Well, unfortunately, a bullet had pierced her below the left collarbone. But she's alright now. She's resting."

Dolly and Arijit were stunned. 'A *bullet wound*?!' They both thought. Just then, a nurse came up to them and said, "The patient has regained consciousness. You may check on her if you wish to. She has been shifted to a private patient's room." Dolly rushed ahead of everybody to see her precious daughter.

Inside the room, Aahuti lay on her bed, her head propped up with two pillows. Dolly hurried to her side and immediately broke down. Carefully hugging her daughter, so as to not irritate her wounds, Dolly sniffled, "How did this happen, love? This guy was telling us that it was a minor accident, and that your Scooty had skidded on the road." Arijit followed suit and rushed in, followed by everybody else. Biplav hesitated by the foot of her bed, overcome with guilt and remorse. Aahuti was shocked to see Biplav; she turned to her mother and screamed, "*Maa*, that's the man that shot me!"

Dolly staggered, completely taken aback by this piece of information. She then put two and two together, and burst into a fit of rage: "This man shot my daughter, and all this while he's been pretending to be an innocent lamb, a hero who rescued her, when the truth is that only he is to blame for her state!" She spat, "He should be handed over to the Police. This is a Police case, and he should be sentenced to jail for attempted murder."

Biplav didn't try to defend himself—he simply said, "Ma'am, I had to lie, because that was neither the time nor the place to tell you both the truth. I am truly sorry. I never intended to hide the truth; I simply delayed it." Unable to control her growing anger, Dolly sneered, "How dare you pretend to be polite and gentlemanly, when you are nothing but a killer—a murderer?"

Sensing the growing discomfort and anger in the situation, Sudha intervened. She said, "Biplav is indeed guilty of a crime, and he *should* be punished for it. However, before any of that, I'd like to tell you why and how the accident really happened." Biplav, looking ashen, slowly walked to the glass window and stared at the scene outside, as the streetlights illuminating the Gulmohar tree. Meanwhile, Sudha recounted his past to Arijit, Dolly, and Aahuti, telling them about how, less than two years ago, Biplav had almost everything that any young man could wish for in his life...

Chapter 3

May 2012

Biplav was a successful professional who had topped his Chartered Accountancy exams when he was just 21 years old. For the last four years, he had been working as the head of the accounts section at Dalmiya Telecommunications. He lived with his elder brother and *bhabhi*, Bishwanath and Sudha, who wanted him to get married to any girl of his choice. It was then that Biplav told them about Koel, a Marwari girl he had been going around with for a while. She was now a colleague of his and was working in the marketing section. An ambitious and career oriented girl, she had just completed her MBA and was a fresh recruit. She joined Dalmiya Telecommunications when Biplav introduced her to Saurabh a few months ago.

Bishwanath and Sudha had no problems with a working Marwari girl, but Biplav told them that Koel wanted to settle in with her career first and thought about getting married later. Sudha had suggested that if she was not against getting engaged, then they could go forth with that and wait for as long as she wanted before tying the knot.

*****

Biplav, Saurabh Dalmiya—the Proprietor of Dalmiya Telecommunications—and Salil enjoyed a bit of male bonding over their evening cup of tea at a crowded roadside tea stall, an activity that was a popular cultural ritual known as *addabaazi* in Bengal. The three guys knew each other since their school days, and were classmates in school until Class 12.

Saurabh belonged to a wealthy Marwari family with a strong business background. Even though he was one of the worst students in the class, and Biplav was one of the brightest, the tables had turned and now, Saurabh was Biplav's boss—a fact he would keep rubbing in Biplav's face mockingly.

During their friendly banter, Saurabh jokingly confessed, "Biplav, I've become very jealous of you ever since you've met Koel. You swooped in and hijacked an incredible marriage prospect from *my* Marwari community." The friends laughed it off, not realising that Saurabh was actually telling them the truth.

Alerting Biplav about Saurabh and his comments, Salil said, "You've made a huge mistake bringing Koel into this company, where a vulture like Saurabh Dalmiya is the boss." On hearing this, Saurabh lost his temper with Salil, while Biplav tried to calm him down.

Refusing to forget the seemingly harmless insult, Saurabh walked off, claiming he had to attend to some important business. Salil complained about Saurabh's inability to take a joke lightly. Biplav laughed and commented, "Look at you both. I'm sure you will forget this bickering soon enough, and find yourselves bonding over a bottle of scotch and taking a trip to Sonagachi."

Salil couldn't deal with Biplav saying such things out loud in public. He scolded, "Do you not care about my reputation?" Biplav couldn't help but laugh over this. Salil then snapped and said, "Listen, I've stopped doing all of that ever since Krutika has come into my life, but Saurabh keeps calling me again and again to join him for some fun." He added, "*Main toh sudhar gaya hoon, magar yeh Saurabh kabhi nahi sudharne waala hai* (I've renounced my ways and become better, but this Saurabh will never improve)."

*****

The next day, Saurabh found a way to express his feelings for Koel when he was alone with her inside his cabin, and went on to propose to her. Politely but firmly, she declined, even as he tried to convince her that Biplav was not well suited for her, and that one day, she'd realise this herself. Annoyed by his persuasion, she stated, "I do not see any point in discussing private matters with my boss," and left him red-faced with embarrassment and anger as she proceeded towards the main office area.

There, Biplav began to click pictures of her with his new cell phone camera. Chintan Ghosh—who also worked in the marketing section, and was very close to Saurabh—came into Saurabh's office to observe the ongoing office romance between Koel and Biplav as he kissed Koel's pictures on his phone screen. Chintan knew that Saurabh was secretly in love with Koel, and encouraged him, saying, "You need to kick Biplav out of the way and marry Koel yourself! After all, a *kangali Bangali* like Biplav doesn't deserve a rich Marwari girl like her."

Fueled by his wounded pride, a sinister plan began to take shape in Saurabh's mind; a plan to get Biplav out of the way. After coming back from their Hong Kong trip, Saurabh confided in Chintan, and Biplav would be forced to let go of Koel forever.

Later that day, while watching a movie at a multiplex, Koel said to Biplav, "You must meet my father as soon as he returns from Hong Kong. I'm up for getting engaged soon and keeping marriage off the cards for now, since my whole family is pestering me to find a nice Marwari boy and get married. At least they'll stop bothering me if I get engaged." "But will your father accept a Bengali son-in-law?" asked Biplav. Challenging Biplav, Koel firmly replied, "To know that, you'll have to meet him for yourself."

*****

A luxury ferry jetted towards Macau from Hong Kong. Aboard the speeding ferry were various groups of people, mostly tourists, in a fun and party-like mood, all bound for Macau, which was known as the Las Vegas of Asia. At the open air restaurant and bar on the deck, Biplav, Saurabh, and Chintan were enjoying some wine with exotic seafood—they were out celebrating the success of their Hong Kong merger deal.

While they were enjoying themselves, Biplav received a call from Koel, and he answered, saying, "Koel! We're all headed for Macau from Hong Kong to let loose and have some fun. Believe it or not, but my *kanjoos* Marwari boss suddenly decided to give us all a treat to rejoice the victory of the merger deal. We plan to stay in Macau for the night, and will

be taking a flight back to Kolkata tomorrow afternoon –"
Just as he was completing his conversation with Koel, loud
music began to play in the background, interrupting his call.

That night, as the three triumphant men entered a casino,
they were greeted by scenes of skimpily clad pole dancers
gyrating to the beats of an item song. They made their way
through one club after another, ogling at the various dancers,
and finally settled on gambling at one of the many casinos.

While everybody tested their luck for the sake of an
experience, Saurabh began to get very involved in the game,
and put a lot of his cash at stake, which eventually led to
him losing a hefty sum. Biplav too lost some money and
decided to call it quits. Chintan neither gambled nor drank,
as his mother hated those things. He played the role of a
full-time supporter and advisor to Saurabh.

After losing out on a considerable amount, Saurabh wished
to keep playing, and wanted more money. He asked Biplav
to withdraw $10,000 from the nearest ATM using his
corporate credit card, but Biplav protested. He retorted,
"Why should I take out money from my account? Why don't
you take out money from your own account?" While Biplav
rambled on agitatedly, Saurabh found himself engrossed at
the roulette table. He laughed off Biplav's concerns, "I'm the
boss of Dalmiya Telecom, aren't I? After all, I would have
to sign the expenditure vouchers myself. We have cracked a
$200 million dollar deal for the company, and we deserve a
treat. What is $10,000?!"

Biplav went and withdrew the money from the ATM using his
American Express card, and handed the amount to Saurabh.

Soon enough, Biplav began to get tipsy, while Saurabh lost again. This time, however, he didn't protest when Saurabh asked him to withdraw another $10,000. Biplav brought back the money and once again, Saurabh loses.

This continued on a few times, by the end of which they were all drunk. Saurabh asked Biplav to withdraw $10,000 again, and this time, he brought back the only money that was left in his company account, since they had exhausted the rest that night.

Now gambling with the last $10,000 from Biplav's company account, Saurabh got an idea. He asked for Biplav's cell phone. Unable to comprehend why Saurabh wanted his phone, he reluctantly handed it over to him. Saurabh scanned the phone and quickly found Koel's picture, and without much ado, kissed Koel's photo for luck. Biplav was shocked. "Come on," teased Saurabh, "Koel is my employee too, and even though you've got her, I still reserve the right to at least kiss her photo for luck in Macau!"

This time, Saurabh won at the roulette table and got very excited. Chintan cheered Saurabh and stopped Biplav from snatching the phone out of Saurabh's hand. Saurabh kissed Koel's photo for luck once more, and the trick worked its charm—he won again. Biplav was growing restless over these actions, and got really upset with Saurabh for doing this. "Come on, man," Saurabh defended himself, "We are in Macau!" Saurabh then repeatedly kissed her photo for luck as a trashy song continued to play in the background.

Saurabh finally won back a lot of money—much more than he'd lost. He felt like the king of the world. Finally, after several hours and multiple rounds of alcohol, the drunken men decided to wrap up and leave. Saurabh finally returned Biplav's phone to him as they stepped out of the casino and into the busy late night streets of Macau.

They found their way back to their hotel room, where they collectively counted their winnings—a whopping total of $80,000! Saurabh then declared, "Since I've won all this money at the casino, this is my own money." Biplav asked for $40,000 so that he could deposit the money back into his company account, but Saurabh said, "Mark everything as office expenditure, and bring me the voucher book so that I can sign it all off right away."

Biplav brought out the voucher book from his room, and filled up 6-7 pages, totalling the amount to $40,000. Saurabh signed one page, but messed up his own signature as his hands were shaking—he was too drunk to even to hold the pen properly.

Biplav mocked him, "Why do you drink so much when you know you can't handle it?" To prove that he himself was not as drunk, despite having drunk the same amount of alcohol as his friend, Biplav signed his name on a piece of paper.

Saurabh was impressed. He suggested, "Biplav, why don't you sign the voucher pages on my behalf? After all, you used to forge my father's (Sri Jagmohan Dalmiya) signature in my diary whenever I used to get red remarks for bad behaviour in school. And remember how for every signature I had to treat you with Rs. 100 worth of sweets—*mishti doi*, *rossogulla*, *kesar sandesh*, etc.?" He continued, "You'd forged *dada's* signature a few times as well."

Challenging Biplav, Chintan taunted, "Forge Saurabh's signature and prove to us that you can keep your hands steady even when you're so drunk." Biplav accepted the challenge and successfully forged Saurabh's signatures on the vouchers. It was evident that he was trying to show off, and Saurabh and Chintan pretended to be very impressed. Saurabh stood up and saluted Biplav to show his admiration for his great capacity to consume so much alcohol and still have the ability to hold a pen steady.

*****

Once they were back in town, Biplav decided to ask Koel's father for her hand in marriage, and get the ball rolling on their impending nuptials. Cold with fear, he sat before a very irritated Roshanlal Zaveri, making several attempts to bring up the subject of his marriage to Koel, but Roshanlal seemed really offended at the thought of having a prospective Bengali son-in-law in a Marwari business family.

Finally, Biplav got down on his knees, pleading to Roshanlal. He was a right sight, and looked as though he was proposing to a girl. It looked so funny, and Biplav looked so pathetic, that Roshanlal bursts out laughing, unable to keep up the strict father act for much longer. Suddenly a bunch of people came out of hiding and made their way into the room, doubling up with laughter.

Biplav was bewildered. Koel rushed in and reprimanded her father, "Papa! Why did you give up the act so soon?!" She was holding a camcorder, and Biplav realised that she had been filming the whole scene between them. Koel's mother was there as well, along with her brother and *bhabhi*. Biplav was shocked to see that Sudha *bhabhi* and Bishwanath *Da* had also entered the room. Like the rest, they too were laughing and having fun at Biplav's expense.

Everybody settled down, and the ladies of the house quickly ordered the servants to bringing in the refreshments for their future son-in-law and his family, as Roshanlal said to Biplav: "*Beta*, Koel drew me up as a very strict father ever since she was a young girl, just so she could keep the boys at bay. This time around however, *I* decided to play the strict father for once, but failed miserably." Everyone applauded his performance, telling him he was fantastic while it lasted.

Koel turned to Biplav and taunted, "I want to keep this recording forever, just to remind you every now and then about how desperate you once were to get married to me." Bishwanath and Roshanlal had already consulted the priests and fixed a date for the engagement, which would soon be followed by the marriage. Biplav and Koel were ecstatic, as was everyone else, especially Sudha.

Finally, Roshanlal announced that he had one grudge with his daughter: "Even when you chose to marry a Bengali, you ended up choosing a CA who will always be calculating money, just like a Marwari. Why couldn't you pick an artist, or singer, or poet? The Bengali community is filled with the like of them, but no—you had to go and find the closest equivalent to a Marwari you could find." Everybody burst out laughing at Roshanlal's self-deprecating sense of humour.

*****

The following morning at the Dalmiya household, a yawning Saurabh, still in his pyjamas, walked out of his house into the lawn where Biplav was waiting for him, seated on a lawn chair. As Saurabh approached him, a servant came and placed a tea tray on the table. Saurabh greeted Biplav, surprised by his Sunday early morning visit, as he sat and began preparing the tea for two.

Right then, Biplav brought out a wedding card and handed it to Saurabh, saying, "This is actually what I am here for." Saurabh is taken by surprise—engaged in a day and married the following week?! Saurabh tried to talk some sense into Biplav, as they had been friends since childhood. He explained, "I honestly don't think this marriage will work out. I honestly think you need to walk away from this marriage and find yourself a nice Bengali girl to settle down with."

Biplav didn't like Saurabh's tone and said to him, "Saurabh, I didn't want to tell you this now, but I've decided to leave Dalmiya Telecomm soon after my marriage." This bit of information made Saurabh furious, and he asked Biplav to resign immediately. Biplav replied curtly, "Well then, I'll have Koel fax you both our resignation letters by lunchtime tomorrow." With that, he stood up, strode across the lawn, and out the front gate.

*****

The next day, as promised, Saurabh's secretary received the faxes of Biplav and Koel's resignation letters. She came in and gave the letters to Chintan, who was sitting with Saurabh. Saurabh laughed at Biplav's stupidity. In a sudden twist of events, he asked Chintan to accept Biplav's resignation and reject Koel's.

That night, the celebrations at Koel and Biplav's engagement were in full swing, and everybody clapped and cheered as they both put the rings on each other's fingers. Champagne bottles were popped and the foam was sprayed all over the couple.

It was then that the Police arrived at the scene and arrested Biplav on charges of embezzlement of company funds, cheating, and forgery—forging his boss Saurabh Dalmiya's signatures on company vouchers. Everybody was stunned. Koel just couldn't believe what she was hearing, and turning to Biplav, she asked, "Is any of this true?" Biplav confessed that while it was true that he had forged Saurabh's signatures on company vouchers, he did it in the presence of Saurabh and Chintan, and he never cheated the company of one single rupee.

Shaken by these new developments, Koel took off the engagement ring and threw it in Biplav's face. She screamed, "You're nothing but a cheat! A fraud!" She stormed out, pushing aside Sudha, who tried to intervene. Roshanlal also asked his guests to leave, as he himself left with his family. The Police handcuffed Biplav and took him away, as Bishwanath sank down to the floor, holding his head.

*****

During Biplav's trial, the most incriminating evidence against him was that of the handwriting expert, who testified that it was none other than Biplav Banerjee who had forged Saurabh Dalmiya's signatures on the company vouchers.

Biplav admitted to having forged Saurabh's signatures, but he went on to say, "Saurabh was testing whether or not I could duplicate his signatures. Please, Sir. I urge you to believe me."

His pleas of innocence were refuted by the prosecution, and Chintan refused to appear as a witness to any occurrence of Biplav forging Saurabh's signatures, at only the latter's insistence and in his presence. Saurabh then turned to the court and said, "Biplav Banerjee has brought shame to a CA's profession by committing this crime against me and my company, and I will appeal to the CA association to cancel his Certificate of Practice."

Unfortunately for Biplav, all the evidence was against him, and he was convicted under IPC sections 420 (for 1 year prison term), 465 (for 6 months prison term), 468 (for 1 year prison term), and 471 (for 1 year prison term), wherein all the prison terms were to be served concurrently. Additionally, a fine of Rs. 30,000 was also imposed on him. Bishwanath and Sudha were crushed and humiliated. As he was being taken to the prison, Biplav threatened Saurabh, "Just you wait till I return. I'm going to make you pay for your evils, Saurabh Dalmiya."

*****

On his return from court after Biplav's trial, Koel came to Saurabh's office and thanked him for not having accepted her resignation letter. That's when Saurabh confessed, "Koel, you should know that I was always concerned about your well-being since the day you joined my company as a Marketing manager. When I got to know about Biplav's wrongdoings in the company, I felt compelled on several occasions to warn you, but unfortunately, I had no evidence to support my claims then. But when I finally did have proof, it was already too late and you were already engaged to that bastard."

She held his hand in gratitude. "No, it's not too late. On the flipside, you saved my life, and I am so grateful that you exposed the real face hidden behind his mask. Saurabh seized the opportunity to confess his feelings again: "Honestly, Koel. I always felt that Biplav was the wrong man for you, and you were treading down the wrong path. Maybe things can change now." Koel lowered her gaze and whispered, "You're right. Maybe things *can* change now," and moved her hand to hold his.

*****

Back in Alipore Jail, it was time for the lights to be put out. Biplav stared rigidly at the iron bars that keep him captive; the barrier that kept him quarantined from the free world. The lights were being turned down for the night one by one, and soon, his face too was hidden by the darkness.

Chapter 4

February 2014

Lying in her bed at the nursing home, Aahuti was listening intently to Sudha, who was telling her about Biplav. Unknown to everybody else, someone else was also present in the room—Rtd. Col. Prasenjit Dutta. At the age of 55, he stood by the open door, listening closely to the tale and keeping an attentive eye on everyone in the room. He was neatly dressed, and stood tall with his long black hair spilling over his shoulders.

Aahuti turned to look at Biplav, who was crouched on the floor with his head between his knees, keeping his face hidden from everyone else. Sudha continued with her story: "Biplav was released from jail just three days ago, and wanted revenge, but instead of hitting Saurabh Dalmiya, the bullet hit you, Aahuti."

"If the bullet had come in contact with her just an inch below," Arijit thought out loud, "she would have died then and there."

Biplav lifted his head to look at Aahuti. "*Kali Ma* did not let that happen because she did not want Biplav to fire any more bullets," Aahuti declared. "If it weren't for her, Biplav would have fired a second or a third bullet," Aahuti continued, "and might have gone to jail again—but this time, for a life sentence for murder. So, honestly, I think I'm lucky for him." Her face breaking into a wide smile, she said, "I just saved you from committing a murder!"

Aahuti then turned to her father and asked, "See, *Papa*? Didn't *Kali Ma* send me to the right place at the right time once again?" Arijit nodded in agreement and patted his daughter's head affectionately. She asked Sudha not to worry, as they weren't going to report the incident to the police, and then teased Biplav, "Unfortunately for you, I cannot guarantee being present the next time you choose to pick up a gun again and shoot Saurabh Dalmiya."

Biplav looked up at Aahuti, his eyes red and swollen from crying. His cheeks and neck were also wet with tears. He moved swiftly and got on his knees, crawling towards the foot of her bed. He realised that it wasn't just her physical features that made Aahuti so beautiful—her warm heart radiated joy, and her forgiving nature made her the most wholesome girl in the world for him. He held on to her feet, and broke down once again, resting his forehead on her feet as he begged for forgiveness. He sobbed, "You don't know how sorry I am. I am truly repentant for having hurt you."

Prasenjit Dutta immediately moved into the room to Biplav, held his shoulders, and pulled him away from Aahuti's feet, asking him not to do this: "I understand. I would have done the same thing had I been in your place, but this is not the right time." Biplav kept pleading and asking for Aahuti's forgiveness. Prasenjit then ordered sternly, "Stop crying like a little baby." His words seemed to have a magical effect on Biplav, and he stopped crying. Aahuti thanked Colonel

Saheb for calming him down and then laid down her conditions: "I'll only forgive him if he promises to throw the very idea of revenge out of his mind."

Everyone looked at Biplav as he stood there, a little shocked over what she had just said. Sudha's eyes filled up and she wiped away her tears. Biplav nodded and made the promise Aahuti asked of him, which finally brought some relief to everyone in the room. Prasenjit patted Biplav on his back and blessed him.

Finally, Dolly had her chance to speak out: "He should be glad that when he fired a bullet, my daughter was there to take a hit. If it was anybody else, I'm sure you would have gone to jail. But my daughter has a big and kind heart—that's why she forgave him so easily, that too with a smile on her face." Prasenjit laughed and exclaimed, "You are right on target this time, Dolly!" Arijit smiled and agreed.

It was then that Bishwanath said, "Now that's everything's sorted, I suggest you leave now, and let Aahuti get some rest. We can all head upstairs to talk." Just as they were leaving, Bishwanath asked if she was hungry, but Aahuti shook her head, saying, "I feel incredibly tired all of a sudden." Bishwanath then asked if she'd like a glass of milk, to which she responded in the affirmative, and he headed off to find a nurse to bring it to her.

The rest of the party made their way upstairs and into the living room. Sudha requested everyone to have a seat. As they settled down, Prasenjit turned to Sudha and asked, "Would it be possible for you to make me some of your wonderful liqueur tea?" Sudha's eyes grew wide in amazement. 'How does he...?' She thought. "Come on," joked Prasenjit, "I don't need to be a face reader to know that—at least 90% of all true blue Bengali women will know how to make fabulous liqueur tea." "So Colonel *Saheb* just made a safe guess," Arijit quipped. They all laughed, and the mood immediately began to lighten up as they relieved themselves of the troubles of the night.

Arijit asked for permission to smoke, but before he could get a response, he brought out his pack of cigarettes. Dolly taunted him, saying, "My husband too, like a true Bengali *bhadralok*, has to have a smoke before tea, with tea, and after tea." Sudha and Bishwanath smiled politely, while Prasenjit let out a loud laugh. Arijit glared at her and then offered a cigarette to Bishwanth as the latter brought him an ashtray, but Bishwanath didn't smoke, and neither did Prasenjit.

Arijit asked Bishwanath, "Can you tell me roughly for how long Aahuti would have to stay here?"

"About ten days," replied Bishwanath.

Arijit then asked about the expenses of the operation and stay, but Sudha interjected, requesting him to not embarrass them by asking this. She said, "We'll take care of everything, and make sure Aahuti is well looked after. She is our responsibility."

Arijit protested, but Dolly sided with Sudha, saying, "If I were in your place, I would have done the same. However, we will send food for her twice a day. We insist." In an attempt to relieve them of any burdens, Sudha pleaded,

"Dollyji, please don't trouble yourselves over Aahuti's meals. I'll prepare her food myself. I assure you, she'll love my cooking."

Later that night, Biplav headed out to bring Aahuti her bag from the Scooty's rear storage. He entered her room just as she was finishing off her glass of milk. The nurse then proceeded to leave with the empty glass, wished her good night and pointed towards a switch by the bed, informing her that she may ring the bell if she needed anything at any hour of the day or night. Biplav placed the bag on the bedside table and said, "I've kept your cell phone inside." She smiled and thanked him.

Biplav wanted to clear the air with her. He said, "I'm not really afraid of serving a second term in prison, but I truly am sorry for having hurt you and putting your life in danger. I've never hurt anybody in my life and I feel very guilty about it." She replied, "I understand. I also know how much you love your *dada* and *bhabhi*, and I understand now that that's why you wanted to clear your name. Unfortunately, you took the plan too far in your attempt to trap Saurabh, and that's why I'm glad that I accidently came in the way to stop him right there." She continued, "I sympathise with you, and I'm sorry for what you've been through in the past."

"Don't you feel bad about what happened with you?" Biplav asked.

"No," she answered, "I'm happy to have been a catalyst in the hands of God. Do you believe in God?"

"I used to," said Biplav, "but I lost faith in God when I was in jail." He continued, "Maybe things will come full circle, and I will turn into a believer once again."

"Maybe?!" she laughed and teased, "Your faith in God hasn't been restored even after meeting me?" Biplav smiled, unable to think of a reply. He just looked into her eyes.

"You look so innocent," she said, "I wonder why your fiancé was unable to see the innocence in your eyes and instead chose to believe in all those who lied about you." Aahuti continued, "She listened to those who were accusing you of a crime you didn't even commit instead of listening to her own heart. If she had given her heart a chance, she would have known the truth; she would have stood by your side."

Biplav tried to think of a comprehensible response and muttered, "Maybe she didn't have a heart; maybe all of this happened to show me just how heartless Koel really was."

Aahuti went on, "If I was in her place, I would never have believed all those false accusations against you, and would have fought them till my last breath to prove your innocence."

In that instant, Biplav felt a sudden, deep connection with her, and looked into her eyes more intently, as though he was in search of the very fountain of emotion and sympathy that made her say what she had just said. There was a sudden spark between them; a sudden and inexplicable urge; a sudden current of attraction to jolt them to attention. Would it be too early to call it love?

She too was unable to look away as she gazed longingly into his eyes. As if hypnotised by her, Biplav took her hand and lifted it to his lips as he got down on his knees to kiss it.

He looked at her and said, "I wish you were in my life in place of Koel." In response, she pulled his hand to her mouth, kissed it, and smiled back at him. "I'm here now, aren't I?" she said. Their breaths seemed to quicken all of a sudden as they were now staring deeply into each other's eyes.

Then, in one swift move, Biplav held her tenderly around her shoulders and kissed her on her lips. She raised her shoulder and moved one hand behind his neck as their mouths melted into each other into a deep and passionate kiss. He moved to hold her tighter and she winced in pain due to her shoulder wound, which made him snap back into his senses. Their kiss ended as abruptly as it had begun, and he stood up with a jerk, feeling all flustered. He mumbled an apology as his eyes darted across the room.

Aahuti giggled, asking, "What are you apologising for now?" He looked back at her to find her gazing at him tenderly. Suddenly blushing, she immediately looked away, and then a moment later looked back at him again. "I-I should leave now," he stammered a little, and left the room. Just as he was about to shut the door behind him, he stopped, took a deep breath, and turned around to look at her. She was looking at him again, but immediately looked away when he caught her eye. He smiled at her. She looked back and held his gaze as she smiled back at him. He shut the door softly. Smiling to herself, she turned on her side, hugged a pillow tight, closed her eyes and fell asleep.

As soon as he left Aahuti's room, Biplav stood in the driveway by her Scooty, looking dazed. He was replaying the last few minutes in his mind, smiling to himself when he heard everyone coming down the stairs. As soon as they spotted him, they approached him on their way to the gate. Prasenjit held him by his shoulders and shook him a bit. "*Beta*, snap out of it! We were all waiting for you upstairs," he said.

"Oh, I had no idea, uncle. I just stepped out for some fresh air," Biplav replied timidly as he walked with them.

Prasenjit said to him, "*Beta*, we have been talking, and we've decided that since Aahuti is going to remain at the nursing home for the next 8-10 days, we are going to need a volunteer in her place to help organise an interactive seminar, which is scheduled to happen in two weeks. I run an NGO— Sanjeevani Institute—which works towards spreading the light of education among the underprivileged, and focuses especially on vocational training, professional courses, and coaching for careers as doctors, engineers, MBA, CA, CS, etc. Since you are responsible for Aahuti being out of action for the next two weeks, we have all decided that you should work in her place and contribute whatever is possible of you."

Biplav didn't like the idea much and protested, saying, "But I have no experience with this kind of work."

Dolly brushed aside his worries and said, "Everybody is a beginner when they first join, but it is better to keep busy with something rather than sit idle."

Sudha agreed with Dolly and added, "Biplav, at least until Aahuti can resume work again, you should consider this your duty to lend a helping hand to Colonel *Saheb*."

Biplav finally gave in and agreed. "So it's all set!" exclaimed Prasenjit. "You could also talk about how you qualified for the CA exams," he said and patted Biplav's back. As he got into the driver's seat of his car, he asked Dolly and Arijit to get inside quickly, since it was already so late and he needed to get some sleep. As the two got in the car, Prasenjit said to Biplav, "Get to my office no later than 10:00 a.m. I've left my office address and number with your *dada*." Biplav nodded. They bid each other goodnight, and just as Prasenjit drove away, Bishwanath gave Biplav a hard stare.

As soon as the visitors had driven away, all of Bishwanath's bottled up anger erupted. He screamed, "It is because of your repeated stupidity that my head is hanging in shame in front of others. First, you got drunk and forged your boss' signatures—how stupid can one get? Then, after a year in prison, you go and shoot a girl. What if I wasn't a surgeon? Then you would have gone to jail again. Why didn't you just come home after you were released? Don't you give a damn about your *dada* and *bhabhi*?"

Sudha made several attempts to calm him down. Bishwanath accused her of having supported Biplav's decision to study for CA instead of becoming a doctor like he wanted. He spat, "If he had become a doctor, he could have helped me run the nursing home. But he wanted to stand on his own feet, to become independent—he wanted to think for himself, and this is what it has all boiled down to." He declared, "Biplav is clearly incapable of growing up and truly stand on his own two feet, and it is all because of you, Sudha. You have spoilt him with your overindulgence and maternal affection."

Sudha ignored his accusations and tried to cheer him up: "Come on, Bishwanath. It's all in the past now. I'm happy that Biplav is finally here with us—isn't that enough? Biplav, please apologise to *dada*."

Biplav just stood there, hurt by Bishwanath's outburst, and reluctant to apologise. "Let it be," Bishwanath said as he stormed off into his room.

Sudha grabbed Biplav's shoulder and ordered him to say sorry. "Your dada will simmer down soon." She looked at his face lovingly and said, "I've missed you very much, Biplav, and I'm so glad you're finally home. As tears welled up in her eyes, Biplav hugged her and replied, "I'm so happy to be home, *bhabhi*. This feels right."

That night, in the privacy of his room, he scrubbed the phone number off his palm. It took some time and effort before the ink faded, leaving behind only a faint smudge.

*****

Aahuti woke up to the sound of birds chirping and smiled to herself. The nurse came in and drew the curtains apart to open the window to let some fresh air in. The flower laden Gulmohar tree outside the window filled her view as she freshened up for the new day, while a neatly dressed, clean-shaven and well groomed Biplav drove to work.

As the day progressed, Biplav and Aahuti went on with their respective lives, each thinking about the other. Over the course of the next few days, Aahuti began to feel better, and her family made frequent visits to check on her. Sudha spent time with her, while Bishwanath checked her wound, and Biplav would meet her as often as he could and would try to kiss her when they were alone, but she'd keep pushing him off playfully.

*****

The day of the seminar drew closer, and Biplav began to get friendly with Aahuti's brother and parents. One day, Biplav finally introduced Aahuti to Salil and his girlfriend Krutika at a coffee shop in South City Mall. Unknown to them, however, somebody was watching them keenly from a distance—it was Chintan.

On spotting them, Chintan informed Saurabh, "I'm convinced that Salil and Krutika have reunited, or they never broke up, because I have seen them together almost every single day." Saurabh was surprised to hear of this. He then realised that Salil had lied to him and laughed at his own stupidity. Chintan also informed Saurabh about Biplav's work with the Sanjeevani Institute, and his involvement in the preparations for an upcoming seminar. He continued, "He's also been going out with this new girl. It seems she was a patient at Sudha Nursing Home where they got to know each other. I saw all four of them together at a posh coffee shop and they seemed to be having a nice time together." Saurabh listened to all this with an evil gleam in his eyes. He wanted to make a thousand little cuts in Biplav's self respect so that he bled to death of humiliation.

*****

Biplav had dinner with Aahuti's family and felt very much at home as he feasted on the delicious fish and sweets that Dolly brought for her. Arijit told him about his family and how his grandfather, a famous barrister, had built this house, so that nobody in the future generations would have to work. They could just sit at home, just as he did, and live on the rental money that came by having so many shops on the ground floor and leasing them out to new businessmen. "All I do is enjoy life—listen to Rabindra *sangeet*, go to cultural programs, fly kites, coach the local football team, and eat and drink to my heart's content. My father too was like that, and I'm hopeful that Jyotirmoi will one day come to his senses and follow in my cherished footsteps," Arijit rambled on.

Biplav found this amusing. Jyotirmoi didn't agree with his father's ideas, and wanted to become a great lawyer like his great grandfather. Biplav supported him, as he found it difficult to accept that a man could just spend all his life in leisure—a man needed to work for self-respect.

Arijit believed the new generation was losing the essence of being a Bengali by giving too much importance to work. "I was born with a lot of self-respect, so I never needed to work for it," he said, "Work is for the proletariat."

"That's why he weighs 110 kilos," Dolly taunted.

"A sign of prosperity," Aahuti quipped, "and also because *Ma* is such a great cook." Biplav agreed to this and complimented Dolly for her cooking.

That night, Aahuti and Biplav were glued to their phones into the early hours of the morning as they whispered sweet nothings to each other. The full moon was visible through his window and he asked her, "Do you notice the pinkish colour of the moon tonight?"

"What rubbish," she scolded him, "How can the moon ever be pink?"

"Look at it. I'm telling you it is," he challenged her.

She walked out to her small open balcony and into the light of the full moon—she found that it indeed seem pinkish. Her balcony was about 5 feet wide and tinier than a small dining table at about 12 feet height from the ground. Finally, Biplav said, "Aahuti, I love you."

Aahuti pretended to be angry and accused him of being out of his mind: "First you kiss me, and then you confess your love, that too under the pretext of being mesmerised by the pink moon!"

Biplav retorted, "I may be out of my mind, but my intentions are noble. And one more thing: I didn't initiate that kiss! That just happened—you made my heart skip so many beats that I got lightheaded and slipped. But after that there never was an opportunity for another kiss."

Aahuti came back with a quick response, "Once is more than enough. Neither have I kissed anyone in the past like that, nor will I do so again in the future."

Feigning hurt over her response, Biplav said, "One kiss in such a long life? That too such a tiny peck?!"

Suppressing her laughter, Aahuti asked, "That was small?" To which Biplav said, "Well, yeah, it was a really short kiss."

In an attempt to pull his leg, Aahuti teased, "You know the long and short of this, but I'm clueless. All I know is that after one, you're not getting another." Their conversation continued, as they teased each other: "Not even if I get your parents' permission to make you mine forever?"

Aahuti understood what Biplav was insinuating, but decided to go along with the charade and said, "What makes you think you'll get away that easily? My father loves me very much; he's not going to let you have me without my consent."

"And what if he asked you about me? Then what will you say?" Biplav retorted.

By now, Aahuti had figured out a way to push his buttons. She simply said, "I'll tell him I have no idea. Biplav never asked me anything—I'd have an answer only if he proposed, wouldn't I?"

Hesitating for a moment, unsure of how to respond, Biplav asked, "Do you love me?"

Feigning disbelief, Aahuti asked, "Are you crazy?! If I didn't love you, I would've slapped you when you came close to me to kiss me!"

Now it was Biplav's turn to take the mickey out of her, "No, I don't care for that explanation. Tell me, do you or do you not love me?"

In a soft voice, Aahuti replied solemnly, "Yes, of course I do."

"You… what?"

"Love you, what else?"

"How much?"

"Now how do I explain that to you?"

Biplav then changed the topic and asked, "Okay, tell me, what are you doing right now?"

Aahuti said nonchalantly, "I'm standing in my bedroom balcony and having this conversation with you."

He then asked, "So if I cut the call now, for how long can you stay there, with your eyes closed, thinking about me?"

Her curiosity growing, Aahuti asked, "You're cutting the call now?"

"Yes."

"And you want me to stand here, in the balcony, with my eyes closed?"

"Yes. Exactly like that."

"For how long?"

"Until I tell you to open your eyes again."

"On the phone?"

Biplav hesitated, so as to not give anything away, "Something like that."

Aahuti paused momentarily and finally said, "Alright, let's see. But if I get dizzy and faint then be prepared to take me to the hospital."

Accepting her condition, Biplav said, "Alright. I'm going to cut the call now."

Right before they ended their conversation, Aahuti said, "You're already crazy, and now, I think I'm going crazy as well."

He cut the call. Shaking her head and smiling to herself, she proceeded to close her eyes and stood there settling in the tranquillity of the night.

Meanwhile, a taxi came to a halt and Biplav stepped out, paid the driver, and nonchalantly walked towards Aahuti's house. As soon as the taxi drove out of sight, his nonchalance gave way to a thief-like stealth as he approached the big gates. He moved along the boundary wall and soon found a spot where he could conveniently climb the wall. He jumped down the other side of the wall and quickly but quietly, moved towards Aahuti's balcony, where she stood with her eyes closed.

He climbed the creepers, managing to find footing in the wall somehow and soon climbed over to the balcony to find her mumbling to herself, "Biplav, would you please call already?! I'm feeling dizzy. If I fall then you watch out. I'll beat you up."

Sitting on the parapet, he grabbed her hand. She shrieked, but he quickly covered her mouth with one hand. She immediately opened her eyes and on recognising Biplav, stopped screaming. He took his hand off her mouth and whispered, "I caught you before you fell, then why are you screeching now?"

Realising his intentions, Aahuti said, "Now I get it! This is why you asked me to stand here with my eyes closed? So you could get here in the middle of the night, like a thief? Have you honestly lost your mind?"

Biplav decided the moment was right and proposed to her. Aahuti was speechless. For a few moments, they stood there, just like that. He kept his eyes locked on her. She looked back at him, but blushed and turned away. He slipped his arms around her waist, drew her closer to him and asked her again: "*Bolo na, mujhse shaadi karogi*? (Tell me, will you marry me?)"

In a hushed voice, Aahuti responded, "Yes."

He tried to get closer to her to kiss her when she abruptly put her hands between them and playfully stopped him.

"No. Not right now. You should go back."

"Just one. A small one. I've come from so far, that too without waking anyone up."

She gave him a quick peck on the cheek and brushed his lips with a light kiss. Biplav said, "That's it? How will this help? Give me one more, but make it longer than the last."

In a stern voice, Aahuti replied, "You're not getting anything more now. Come speak to my father in the morning and then make me yours. You'll get whatever you want only after that."

He accepted her condition, kissed her hand, and began to climb back down. She kept looking at him with a smile on her face and waved goodbye.

*****

The day of the seminar finally arrived. The Pavillion Hall—where the event was to be held—stood tall and proud adjacent to the Rabindra Sarobar. Large banners were hung outside the auditorium as the rumble of the activity inside was heard. Inside the auditorium, present hundreds of adolescents and adults were engrossed in the interactive session. Many scholarly looking men and women were present on stage with Prasenjit. Aahuti was there too.

A teenager holding a microphone asked Biplav a question about CA and as Biplav was answering the question, the mic was snatched from the boy's hands by Chintan Ghosh, who passed it on to Saurabh Dalmiya sitting next to him. Saurabh interrupted Biplav, blasting him: "You're nothing but a criminal who looted the very company you worked at as a CA, went to jail for a year and now, here you stand, telling these boys about the secret to qualifying for CA! Instead, you should conduct sessions on how to commit forgery, financial crimes, and how to stab one's boss in the back. You're nothing but a rotten apple who will lead to the rotting of these innocent minds."

Biplav was stunned by this sudden ambush, and many in the audience joined Chintan and Saurabh as they attempted to boo Biplav off the stage. Prasenjit came to Biplav's rescue and tried to control the situation, but the anger directed at Biplav soared and suddenly, a slipper came hurtling towards him and hit him in the face. Prasenjit lost his temper at this and strongly chastised the unruly crowd as Biplav stood there, shell-shocked. Aahuti rushed to Biplav, took his hand, and walked him out of the venue towards the lake.

Biplav was hurt and shaking in anger. The thoughts of revenge were once again flooding his mind. 'It was a mistake to let go of a bastard like Saurabh. Vipers like him do not deserve to be let off the hook and should be crushed,' he fumed inwardly.

Aahuti pacified him, sympathised with him, and tried to motivate him. She reminded him of the meaning of his name—Biplav meant 'revolution' in Bengali. She reminded him, "You're one of the youngest Chartered Accountants in the country. Even if they had the power to throw you in jail for a crime you didn't commit, and to take away your CA license, they do not have any power to take away your brilliant mind and pure heart. If only you'd wake up to your full potential, then you'd become a guiding light, akin to a lighthouse, directing the lost souls in the right direction."

Biplav confessed that he felt alone and weak, to which she said, "You are not alone. You have me, and you will always have me."

As she held his hand, reassuring him, he asked, "Will you stand by me through everything? Through all the ups and downs? Will you hold my hand forever and never let go, not matter what?"

Aahuti remained silent for a minute before she nodded and said, "Of course I will. I vow to be by your side through thick and thin. You're *my* man now, and you will always be the only man in my life."

They made their way to a *Kali Ma* temple in the vicinity. Aahuti stepped inside to seek *Kali*'s blessings. When she saw that Biplav wasn't paying his respects properly before the idol, she grabbed him by the collar and brought him down next to her. Biplav surrendered and prayed to the idol. They seemed like the happiest couple in the world as they stepped out, and Biplav's heart was filled with joy as the veil of gloom surrounding him finally seemed to be gone forever.

*****

While the happy couple went about their lives blissfully, in another part of town, a pathologist was testing a blood sample using sophisticated equipment. The blood showed the presence of antibodies, and the pathologist marked the sample as HIV+.

Golmes matched the blood sample number against the entries in the log book and his forefinger came to a stop at Biplav Banerjee's name and signature. His face was suddenly drained of all colour and he began to perspire.

*****

Back at the Sanjivani headquarters, the atmosphere was filled with a sense of camaraderie and bonhomie as the staff settled for lunch. Aahuti and Biplav were lost in their own world and she was making plans for their marriage. She asked him to talk to his *dada* and *bhabhi* about his intention to marry her. "Once they have agreed to the union, they should come meet my parents to talk about it," she said.

Biplav agreed to the plan, but he was a little concerned: "I'm not sure if your parents would be willing to accept a son-in-law who has spent time in prison, and has no career left to speak of after losing his CA license."

In that moment, Prasenjit, who had been eavesdropping on them, came into view and said, "I think your mother will be okay with the marriage. After all, Biplav, you are an educated, intelligent, and handsome young man, and your brother owns a nursing home, three cars, and a big house." He continued, "She believes that you can easily set up any business you want at any time, and she'd love to have you as a son-in-law. I'm sure nobody will come in your way if you have decided to tie the knot."

Hesitating, Biplav asked, "What if, a few years after marriage, when our children go to school, somebody tells them that their father was once sentenced to a year-long jail sentence because of a crime he committed? Moreover, if an incident like the one at the seminar takes place at the wedding, then what will we do?"

Giving his queries a thought, Prasenjit reassured him, "I'll handle both those situations, if and when they arise. Don't worry too much."

Prasenjit then walked into his cabin as he called someone using his cell phone. He shut the door carefully as he spoke into his phone: "… yes, his name is Chintan Ghosh. He works at Dalmiya Telecomm—yes I want all his personal details, all the information one can get about him."

*****

A worried looking Matthew Golmes—the Director of the blood bank that stored the blood that now ran through Aahuti's veins—walked up to the reception at Sudha Nursing Home, where at least half a dozen patients were waiting with their relatives to see the doctor. Golmes asked for Jhantu. When the receptionist told him that Jhantu was out running errands, Golmes presented his visiting card to the receptionist and said, "I need to see Dr Bishwanath urgently." The receptionist took the card, and entered Dr Bishwanath's cabin. Inside, Dr Bishwanath was examining a patient when the receptionist handed the card to him. Dr Bishwanath glanced at the card and asked her to send in Mr Golmes next.

While in his cabin, Golmes broke the news to Bishwanath. His voice weighed down by sorrow, he told him that a regular blood donor had been found to be HIV+, and it was suspected that the blood he donated over the past couple of months might be HIV+ too. He explained to Bishwanath about the 'window period' of 2-3 months, during which time even if the virus might be present in the blood, the routine blood tests for antibodies would not be able to detect its presence. "It was blood from this donor that was sent to your nursing home about a month ago, and I'm almost certain that whoever was administered that blood would be HIV+ too by now," he said.

Unable to accept this new development, Bishwanath remained frozen, shaken to the core as he absorbed this piece of information. Golmes produced a letter printed on the Arogya Blood Bank's letter pad and signed by him, accepting the blunder committed by the blood bank. It was a grave case of human error.

Golmes said, "I desperately wish my blood bank had the machines to be able to detect HIV virus in blood samples even during their window period, but those machines are too expensive and are available at only a few hospitals in countries like ours. This document can help the girl if she wishes to sue us for compensation, but I hate to say this at the risk of sounding selfish, it can also make me lose my job. However, I still felt ethically bound to prepare and bring this letter to you." As Golmes spoke, Bishwanath could feel insides churning as he stared at the paper, hoping on hope that this was all just a dream.

During dinner that night, Biplav kept probing Sudha to talk to *dada*, but Sudha kept playfully urging him to talk to his *dada* himself. Bishwanath asked gravely, "What is going on between the two of you?"

Sudha nudged Biplav, "Out with it already."

Biplav looked into his *dada's* eyes with confidence and said, "*Dada*, Aahuti and I are in love, and we wish to get married. I'd really appreciate it if you and *bhabhi* would go to her parents and ask for their permission to let me marry her."

All colour drained from Bishwanath's face as he heard this, and he could do nothing but sit there, shocked and numbed. Finally he exploded, "Have you two gone mad?!" He immediately jumped off his seat, leaving his meal midway, and stormed into his bedroom.

Sudha and Biplav sat there in shock, wondering what happened to Bishwanath. Biplav felt more confused than dejected at his *dada's* reaction and pleaded to Sudha to find out what objection *dada* had to this marriage. Sudha reassured him, saying, "Calm down, Biplav. I'll speak to your *dada* tonight itself."

While Biplav paced the length and breadth of his room, he grew restless with each passing minute as he heard the faint voices of Sudha and Bishwanath coming from their bedroom. He came out and tiptoed to their bedroom door to eavesdrop on their conversation. Inside, Bishwanath kept trying to avoid Sudha's question: "Why are you against

Biplav marrying Aahuti? I think you're hiding something from me and I want an answer now. This is our brother we're talking about."

Bishwanath couldn't rein it in any longer. He blasted, "There is 100% possibility that Aahuti is now HIV+ because one among the three pouches of blood brought for her that night was infected with HIV." He brought out the document from a folder and handed it to Sudha, telling her he got to know of it only today. Sudha was shocked and speechless as she stared at the paper she was holding.

Just then, Biplav burst into the room, shaking all over because of the shocking news. He exclaimed, "I refuse to believe this. I'll get Aahuti's blood tests done myself." Biplav took the results from Sudha's hands as he shuffled out of the room, his head spinning from all the new information.

*****

The next morning, as Aahuti was preparing to leave for work, she was surprised to find Biplav in her living room, chatting with the rest of her family, who told her that he'd arrived a few minutes ago. "I was in the neighbourhood for some work, and figured I would pick you up on the way to office." They left the house together, as Biplav racked his brain to find a suitable way to break the awful news to the woman he loved. Completely unaware of all that was to unfold, Dolly and Arijit both looked on, thinking about how the kids made a great couple and were well suited for each other.

While on their way to work, Biplav hesitated before he told Aahuti of the mix-up at the blood bank. He said, "Aahuti, there's no easy way for me to say this, but there's a definite chance that you're HIV+. I had to lie to your parents about taking you to work, because I'm actually taking you to Appolo Gleneagles Hospital to get you tested. I refuse to believe this, and I want to see test results myself before I can accept this."

Aahuti felt her throat close up. She didn't know what to think or say. She grimly read the document Biplav handed to her, unsure of how she was supposed to feel. She sat there, staring at the paper in her hand, as they approached the hospital.

Biplav raced Aahuti into the hospital. They approached the receptionist, who directed them to the HIV/AIDS Counsellor. Inside the Counsellor's cabin, Biplav and Aahuti were advised to take a rapid test for the HIV antibodies, the results for which would come through in a matter of 30 minutes. They thanked her and made their way into the pathologist's lab, where the nurse took a blood sample from Aahuti for testing.

The next thirty minutes were some of the most nerve-wracking moments of their lives. As they waited, the nurse delivered the results to the Counsellor, who then called Biplav and Aahuti to show them the report. In a grave voice, she said, "I'm sorry to say this, but Aahuti, the report concludes that you are, in fact, HIV+." Aahuti didn't react. She just sat in her chair, frozen.

The Counsellor continued, "There are times when the rapid test delivers false negative results, but in your case, since there already is a history of contaminated blood transfusion, there is no need for a regular antibody test done to be absolutely certain. If you want, I can have a regular antibody test done." She continued, "However, even if that test reports positive, it doesn't mean a death sentence at all. With proper and regular treatment, you can easily live a long life and can even have HIV- children under medical supervision."

Aahuti suddenly stood up and left. Just as Biplav stood up to run after her, the Counsellor said, "Look after her, and keep a close watch on her. She needs to be handled sensitively, as she might be feeling suicidal or like running away. Right now, she is in a state of shock and she will feel better if she finds a way to express her emotions. Bring her back to me when she's ready." Finally, she said, "Nobody should force her to take any decision, and nobody, not even her parents, should be told about her condition without her permission." Biplav nodded and thanked her before he rushed to catch up with Aahuti.

Biplav ran to the parking lot, where he found Aahuti leaning against his car. He approached the vehicle and unlocked the doors, while Aahuti grabbed the document from the blood bank and tore them to bits. "Why did you do that?!" Biplav exclaimed. "It could have helped us file a case against the blood bank and sue them." Aahuti replied, her voice laced with malice, "Yes, and when the investigation would begin, they'd discover that the operation was done for the extraction of a bullet fired by a certain Biplav Banerjee. Also, your *dada* went ahead with the operation without involving the Police; an act that could get him into major trouble."

Aahuti paused to catch her breath. Before she continued, she hesitated as she attempted to come to terms with a decision she had made as soon as she walked out of the Counsellor's office. She finally said, "I love you and want you to live a long and safe life. That's why I've decided that I need to move away from you. You need to forget about me, and rid your mind of all thoughts of me. You need to find a healthy girl and marry *her*." She made her point and began to walk away.

Biplav realised what she meant and followed her. He caught hold of her arm and declared, "I'm never letting you go. You can't make me." Aahuti threatened to kill herself if he didn't let her go. A shocked Biplav let go of her arm and watched her walk away from him. Aahuti found her way to the main road and hailed a cab to take her home as Biplav watched on. Inside the vehicle, Aahuti sat still; her mind as blank as her eyes.

She asked the driver to take her to Rabindra Sarobar, where she sat quietly by herself on a bench, oblivious to the flurry of activity around her, as though she was in a trance. Her brain filled with more thoughts and emotions than it could compute, she sat still, holding back, unable and unwilling to show her feelings. As she watched time go by, she was distracted every now and then by her ringing phone which flashed Biplav's name.

On the other end of the line, a frantic Biplav tried over and over again to get in touch with Aahuti, but to no avail. He finally gave up, but was unable to rid himself of that sinking feeling and that nagging question that kept knocking at his soul: 'Where is Aahuti?' One of his colleagues, Varsha, a lady in her 40s, came to him with her mobile phone, saying the Colonel *Saheb* wanted to speak with him. Biplav took the phone and spoke to Prasenjit, who was on his way to the Sanjivani office after having received his guest, Mr Ardeisher Irani, a well-known industrialist in his 70s, at the airport. He said to Biplav, "I have been trying to get through to you for the last half hour, but you seemed to be on another call. To top it off, Aahuti isn't answering her phone either. What's going on?"

In an attempt to steer away from the truth, Biplav made some excuse and asked Prasenjit about the plan. Prasenjit narrated, "Unfortunately, Mr. Irani's flight was 20 minutes late. But not to worry; we're on our way as we speak. First, as planned, Mr. Irani will come to the office, have lunch there, and then we will all proceed to have a look at the three sites. We'll finalise one of those three before Mr. Irani leaves for his return flight to Mumbai this evening." Prasenjit then asked, "Biplav, can you make sure everything goes according to plan, since we do not have a minute to waste, considering Mr. Irani is here only for a few hours."

Biplav assured him that it will be so. Prasenjit then said, "Now that we're done with our talks of business, tell me— what happened to Aahuti?"

Biplav said, "She's not feeling very well, so she's resting so she gets better as soon as possible. I apologise on her behalf."

Amused by his last statement, Prasenjit joked, "Oh come on, why are you saying sorry for her?! You are supposed to become one soul in two bodies after your marriage. Just ask her to take some medicine if it's not very serious." Stating that he would reach the office in an hour's time, if Kolkata traffic permits him, Prasenjit disconnected the call.

*****

While still at Rabindra Sarobar, Aahuti made every attempt to distract herself from the situation. She glanced around at all the life blooming around her. She noticed a couple of squirrels as they chased each other up and down the trees and across the grass. They soon caught her attention and she was diverted from her gloomy thoughts as she watched the play with amusement. She began to notice other life forms around her—butterflies drawing nectar from the flowers, birds welcoming the approaching evening with their young ones, people engaged in animated conversations in the distance, lovers nuzzling into each others' ears, kids playing, infants learning to walk… the whole world seemed to be abuzz, and she began to see the eternal flow of life in all the activities around her.

Aahuti snapped out of her daze and wiped away the tears welling up in her eyes. She tried to distract herself again by playing a game on her mobile phone. Just then, she received a call from home, her mother's name flashing on the screen. Making every attempt to sound busy and nonchalant, she mumbled into the phone, "I'm very busy right now, *Ma*. I'll call you back later."

Before Aahuti could disconnect, Dolly quickly said, "I'm just calling to ask if Biplav's coming to dinner this evening. I'm stepping out to run some errands, so I just wanted to know if I should buy Hilsa fish for him."

Aahuti hesitated and said, "Yes. Biplav and I will be home by 07:00 p.m."

"Good," replied Dolly, and disconnected the call. As soon as she drew the phone away from her ear, more tears flowed from Aahuti's eyes, and no number of attempts to curb them sufficed.

*****

Prasenjit entered his office with Mr. Irani, showed him around, and introduced him to Biplav and the other staff. He then asked about what happened to Aahuti. Biplav responded, "I picked her up this morning, but she began to feel sick soon after, so I left her at Salil's house to rest it out."

Prasenjit found this strange. He said, "She should have just gone back home then. Or, she could have just come to office and rested here."

Biplav continued with his lie and said, "Salil's house is actually on the way, and so I figured Aahuti could rest there and then come to work by afternoon if she felt better. I've just called Salil's mother, and she mentioned that Aahuti was still asleep."

"Fine," said Prasenjit. Rubbing his hands excitedly, he said, "Now come on, let's all quickly have lunch and then proceed to the sites."

*****

Soon after she spoke to her daughter, Dolly headed out to the market to buy Hilsa at the fish market, bargaining fiercely like all true-blooded Bengalis. A thought suddenly occurred to her and she fished out her cell phone from her handbag to call Biplav, who was with Prasenjit and Mr. Irani at the time. They were driving through the streets of Kolkata in a Qualis with a few other members of the staff. When Biplav answered, Dolly asked, "Biplav, do you prefer fried Hilsa or the one with curry?"

Taken aback by the random question, Biplav remembered his dinner plans with the Senguptas later that evening. Dolly said, "I assumed you may have forgotten, so I thought I should remind you and confirm the plan. You're coming, aren't you?"

"Oh yes," Biplav stuttered nervously, "I actually don't mind the fish either way—fried as well as with gravy."

Dolly responded happily, "Great! I knew it," and disconnected the call.

Prasenjit began to hum an old film song to tease Biplav. Everybody laughed along with him, but Biplav's face said otherwise. His expression betrayed him and Prasenjit noticed his lips quivering with nervousness. He patted Biplav's shoulders and comforted him, saying, "Don't fret. She'll be alright soon. You shouldn't worry about her so much."

*****

The party soon reached the final site. Prasenjit, Mr. Irani, Biplav, and the others moved around inside a building where the interiors had been designed into large classrooms. Mr. Irani seemed impressed and decided, "This site is better than the last two we looked at. There is enough space here so that I can also shift my office to this place." Prasenjit concurred. Looking through the large window from where the entrance to the two storey building was visible, Mr. Irani commented, "The large open space in the front would be great for the kids to park their bicycles and bikes."

Biplav interrupted and remarked, "This place is also much more expensive than the other two."

Mr. Irani didn't see that as a problem; he said, "I want to pay for the best. I want Colonel Dutta to have the best location for his institute, where he can light the fire of knowledge in the minds of the teenagers of this country."

Prasenjit felt as though Mr. Irani was flattering him unnecessarily, saying, "Well, sir, I'm only trying to do something worthwhile for the world we live in."

Mr. Irani grabbed him by the shoulders and said, "No my friend, I have always known that you are a revolutionary at heart, and I believe in your dream."

He then asked Prasenjit to negotiate for that place and let him know the amount. "I'll have the money transferred to your account right away."

Prasenjit interjected, "Oh no, sir. That won't do. You will have to come here for the inauguration of the institute as well." Mr. Irani hesitated but finally accepted the invitation on one condition—the day of the inauguration should also coincide with the Colonel's birthday, which was just round the corner. Flattered that Mr. Irani remembered his birthday, Prasenjit accepted his condition.

*****

Sitting quietly by herself, Aahuti suddenly heard the sound of the daily evening *aarti* in the distance. She turned in the direction of the soft music and listened to the *aarti* for a few moments. There was a Kali temple in the distance, where the evening *aarti* had just begun. Aahuti felt as though the deity was calling out to her. She got up and began to walk towards the temple as the ritual reached its usual frenzy of sound and chanting and then transposed into a devotional song of Maa Kali sung by all the people present there.

Aahuti stepped inside the temple and joined the other devotees. As the *aarti* progressed, she seemed to get overwhelmed by the Kali idol and involved herself in the ritual. She too began to sing and sway while clapping her hands, as the tears began to flow from her eyes. She got closer to the idol, knelt down, and pressed her forehead on the platform. Soon, her body began to convulse and shake as tears from deep inside began to flow. She sobbed to the idol, asking the deity, "Why did I have to leave the man I loved? Why did it have to be this way?"

*****

Biplav was on his way to the airport with Prasenjit to see off Mr. Irani when he got a call from Aahuti. He almost jumped in his seat when he saw her name flashing on the screen. Taking the call, he almost stammered as he asked her how she was feeling now. She replied, "I'm walking down Park Street and am much calmer now. I'm feeling better. I called to tell you that I'll wait for you at the Park Street Oxford bookstore, since *Ma* is expecting you to come home for dinner."

Unable to gauge her mood, he said, "But I'm on my way to the airport with Colonel *Saheb* to drop Mr. Irani."

Suddenly, Prasenjit asked the driver to stop the vehicle on the side of the road. He leaned over and opened the door on Biplav's side and asked him to get out. Biplav sat there, shocked, but Prasenjit repeated his order. Biplav got out of the vehicle. Prasenjit then ordered, "Go straight to Aahuti and enjoy the Hilsa—us oldies will have a drink at the airport." He chuckled at the expression on Biplav's face and asked the driver to proceed.

Watching the vehicle drive on, Biplav quickly hailed a taxi and called Aahuti. He mumbled, "I'll pick you up from the Park Street Oxford bookstore in 30 minutes. From there, we'll first go to the Sanjivani Institute and take my car, and then head to your house," and disconnected the call before Aahuti could respond.

The taxi stopped right in front of the bookstore and Biplav got out, asking the taxi driver to wait for a few minutes, and hurried inside. As he walked in, he saw Aahuti paying for a book and went to her. He was staring at her, but she avoided looking at him as she accepted the change from the cashier. "Where were you all day? Why didn't you take my calls? Do you realise how tense I was all day while lying and pretending to everybody that everything was fine? I kept thinking of the worst all the time," Biplav complained. In a calm tone, she asked him to lower his voice.

Biplav looked at the book she had bought—it was 'The Path of the Mystic Lover: Baul Songs of Passion and Ecstasy'. He turned the book over and commented, "Seems like it would make for an interesting read."

Aahuti replied, "I never expected to find this. I guess it's my lucky day today. I've bought it as a birthday gift for Colonel *Saheb*."

She proceeded to tell Biplav of a story the Colonel had once narrated to her: "He was talking about this book a few months ago, and told me how much he wanted to read it as he was very interested in the philosophy and lives of the Bauls. He told me he once ran away from home as a kid and went to live with the Bauls after meeting them at a village fair. His father somehow traced him and brought him back after he was missing for eight months, and gave him a crew cut, chopping off all his long hair. Poor Colonel *Saheb* didn't stop crying for three days."

Aahuti couldn't help but giggle as she imagined Prasenjit's father cutting off his long locks and him crying. She continued, "His father made him join the army. The Colonel also won a medal in the Kargil war, but after his father died he lost interest in the army life. Finally, he retired because they did not allow him to grow his hair long like the Bauls and even now, he wants to leave everything and go live a wandering life with the Bauls someday." Biplav's mind was elsewhere and he held her hand as he directed her towards the exit.

He brought her to the waiting cab and directed her to get in. Once inside and on their way to her house, Biplav turned to her and hugged her tight. "Where were you? Why didn't you answer my calls?" Returning his embrace ever so slightly, she said, "I needed to spend some time alone," and slowly let go of him. He tried to hold her again but she stopped him, asking him to not approach her again. There was a certain determination in her voice, her eyes, and her body language that Biplav hadn't seen before.

"Why?" he asked. She replied curtly, "Hereon, I'm never going to allow you to come close to me again. If you truly love me, you will respect my decision and leave me be." Biplav kept staring at her, dumbstruck by the condition she had just presented.

"Do you love me?" she asked.

"Yes," he said.

"Then promise me that you will never touch me again," she spoke firmly.

No reply.

After a few moments, he asked her if she truly loved him. She replied in the affirmative, and went on to say, "But love is not restricted to physical acts; when two people fall in love, it is a union of two souls. In true love, these two souls become one."

Biplav butted in with a counter-argument and said, "Then they become one soul living in two bodies, and so, it is only natural that the two bodies also want to experience the same oneness that is being experienced by the soul."

Aahuti fell silent and her determination weakened. Her emotions took hold of her once again. "I will never stop loving you—body, mind, and soul—just because of the fear of death," Biplav told her. Once again, she didn't react to his words and looked away. He moved closer to her and held her tight as he pulled her face towards his and kissed her full on her lips. She resisted and struggled, but he refused to let her go and kissed her deeply. She strove hard and eventually freed herself from his firm grip. Panting hard and looking furious, she managed to control herself and warned Biplav, "If you ever, EVER do that again, and if you ever cross your limits, then I will leave everything behind—you, my family, my home, my job, my city—and move away forever."

Her threat seemed too serious to be ignored. Biplav couldn't do much else but look at her, panting hard as well. He made an attempt to convince her that touching, hugging, or even kissing didn't spread HIV/AIDS, but even though Aahuti knew all this very well, she still pushed him away and refused to let him approach her. The taxi driver, however, overheard all this and became suspicious and terribly scared that his passengers were AIDS patients. He asked worriedly, "Are-are you HIV/AIDS patients?" Biplav asked him to focus on driving the vehicle and mind his own business. In response, the taxi driver veered the taxi to the side of the road and stopped. In a polite but assertive tone, he said, "You're going to have to find another cab. My car has broken down and won't be able to go any further."

Biplav lost his temper and began to argue with him, but the driver refused to budge. Aahuti got out and pulled Biplav along with her, asking him to calm down. "What's the harm if we catch another taxi? Let it go," she said. Biplav gave up and took out money to pay the taxi driver, but the fellow refused the money, scared to even touch it, fearing that the notes may infect him with the disease. Shaking his head, he said, "I don't want your money. Please go. Go!"

Aahuti dragged Biplav by his arm and they both began to walk down the road as they looked for another taxi. Biplav silently cursed the driver, making Aahuti laugh. "What is the use of swearing at that fellow?" said Aahuti, "he was only reacting the way any normal person would. Not many people will come near me now if they find out I'm HIV+, irrespective of whether they are friends or strangers. Gosh, I shudder to think what will happen if people in my neighbourhood and workplace come to know about this."

Biplav replied, "The best solution would be to keep it a secret, then."

She agreed: "We must also pretend that everything is normal between us." She continued, "Else somebody might become suspicious, and I don't want my family to know of my condition, because the news will destroy them."

It was Biplav's turn to agree with her. They finally decided that just between them, they would continue to be only good friends. That's when Biplav said, "On one condition. You meet the Counsellor and seek treatment from an HIV/AIDS doctor." She accepted his terms just as a taxi halted right before them.

Soon after they were on their way to her house in the new cab, she said, "In some time, you and I will start picking on each other, develop irreconcilable differences, begin to argue and fight with each other, and eventually break up, all as per our plan." Biplav nodded in agreement, feeling helpless; he was left with no choice but to agree with her.

*****

That night at the Sengupta household, Dolly, Arijit, Jyotirmoi, Aahuti, and Biplav were all seated at the dining table, enjoying a hearty meal. Biplav feasted on the Hilsa that Dolly had specially prepared for him. She then broached the topic of his marriage, egging him on to get married soon. Biplav said, "Yes, I do believe I should. As soon as I possibly can."

Aahuti, unwilling to let this discussion continue, interrupted him and said, "Rather than spending your time thinking about your marriage, you should work towards getting back on your feet and build your career. Since you can no longer practice as a Chartered Accountant, you need a new direction in life." She continued, speaking with an air of finality, "You should consider your time at the NGO as nothing more than a temporary arrangement."

Dolly didn't like the way Aahuti preached to Biplav and admonished her. "Well I'm sorry, but the truth *is* bitter," Aahuti shouted back.

In an attempt to douse a fire before it had a chance to burn, Biplav interjected, "No, Aahuti is right. Which is why, I'm getting into the teaching business and will be teaching aspiring CAs at the Sanjivani Institute. I will be teaching there as nothing more than an employee of the NGO, but I can also opt to teach independently at coaching institutes and make a lot more money than I could have made as a CA."

"So then find a girl who will be willing to marry an ex-convict who has spent time in jail," Aahuti taunted. Shocked by her daughter's audacity, Dolly's anger flared and she blasted

Aahuti for insulting a guest like this. "Why get angry at me?" Aahuti burst out laughing, "you should be ashamed of yourself. Now I realise why you wanted to invite him for a Hilsa feast." Aahuti doubled over with laughter and said, "You wanted to lure him into marrying me, didn't you?" She teased, "Come on, mom, Biplav is just a good friend of mine, and if you had asked me earlier I would have told you so, and you wouldn't have needed to treat him to Hilsa." Jyotirmoi too began to laugh and soon, Arijit followed suit. Dolly was very pissed. Biplav, however, could see the pain behind Aahuti's laughter.

*****

In the brightness of daylight, the bare structures of many pandals being constructed for the upcoming Durga *puja* could be seen along the roads, in parks, and other open spaces as Biplav drove Aahuti to meet with the Counsellor.

Soon after they got to the hospital, they were ushered into the Counsellor's cabin, where she asked them if they would like to see a doctor at a hospital or at a private clinic. "A private clinic would be better," said Biplav.

Aahuti wondered out loud, "Why? Wouldn't a private clinic be way more expensive?"

"It would ensure privacy and secrecy," Biplav said in an authoritative tone.

The Counsellor advised, "You should see a doctor on the other side of the city, as there would be a lesser chance of any acquaintance spotting you there. I recommend Dr. Balraj Chugani—here's his personal mobile number."

She handed them a card with the doctor's details. "He attends to patients in 2-3 hospitals across the city, but he also meets with some patients in his private clinic, for those who can afford it."

Biplav assured her that money wouldn't be a problem for Aahuti's treatment. She then mapped out the route to his clinic for them: "The address for his private clinic near Joka is not printed on any visiting card, neither is registered in the Yellow Pages, so there's no way you can get there without following my instructions. I'll call him up and brief him about Aahuti's case and get you an appointment with him right away."

*****

Biplav and Aahuti soon fell into a routine, with Biplav picking her up for office every day. After they'd both leave, Dolly grew suspicious about the real deal between them. Biplav looked very devoted to Aahuti, but it was her daughter that Dolly was full of doubt about. On one hand, she humiliated him and then on the other hand, she said he was a good friend. "He is such a good boy," Dolly sighed, "where will she find a guy like Biplav?"

She asked Arijit to talk some sense into his daughter. Trying to lure his wife out of her thoughts, Arijit said, "I find nothing out of order with Aahuti. Dolly, let them take their time. They have only known each other for four months, and it's better if they become good friends before they decide to tie the knot." He continued, "I do, however, agree with you. Aahuti will not find a better match for herself than Biplav."

*****

Biplav came out of a pathology lab with reports and got into his car, where Aahuti waited patiently. He then drove them to Dr. Chugani's clinic, passing several pandals in different phases of construction. Aahuti wondered what Prasenjit would make of the two of them taking breaks from work so frequently. "Being absent from work for a few hours is better than being away from home because then, your mother will get suspicious," Biplav observed.

"Would it be better to tell Colonel *Saheb* about all that's happening," wondered Aahuti, "I am sure he will understand."

Biplav said, "I'm sure he'll understand, and one day, he will have to be told the truth, but I don't think the time is now."

They finally arrived at the private clinic. They waited in the reception area before they were summoned, and made their way into the consultation room. Dr. Balraj Chugani was a slim, practical man in his early 50s. Behind his businessman-like manners, there was a man who cared deeply for his patients. He checked Aahuti's reports and mumbled along, "Your CD4 count is 870, which is normal. It will begin to drop in some time. The purpose of medication is, primarily, to not let this drop below 400 to 300. We will keep a watch on the CD4 count by testing your blood every 15 days, and there is no need to start medication until it drops below 500/micro litre." He noticed the confusion on Biplav and Aahuti's faces and explained what CD4 was.

"You know, to be honest, at my age of 52, if I am given a chance today to choose between two terminal diseases— cancer or HIV/AIDS—then I would choose to have HIV/

AIDS, because cancer will certainly kill me in a few years at the most, but I can live well into my senile years with HIV/AIDS if I look after myself." He went on to say, "Nowadays, it is not difficult to live well into old age with HIV/AIDS if the patient is properly medicated and follows their medicine schedule properly. Taking the medicines regularly is very, very important because one has to go on taking the medicines day after day, week after week, year after year, for several years. It is here that many patients give up, because a sense of futility overpowers them and then they succumb to the effects of this deadly disease."

Dr. Chugani stopped to observe them for a few moments and then asked if they had any marriage plans. They replied together: "Yes," said Biplav, and Aahuti muttered, "No."

Dr. Chugani laughed and said, "Well, whatever you do that is up to you." He then said gravely, "However, it is my duty to warn you that any sexual contact, even just once, between you and a healthy man might infect him with HIV as well, and even though condoms reduce the risk to a great extent, they do not give a 100% guarantee. If you do get married to a healthy man, then I would recommend a marriage without sex." Dr. Chugani sighed, "Opt for artificial insemination if you want children."

Biplav asked curiously, "Doctor, do you know of any couples wherein only one partner is HIV+?"

"Yes," answered Dr. Chugani, "I know many such couples." Biplav's eyes lit up at this information. "In most cases," Dr. Chugani added, "the other partner gets infected with HIV sooner or later. In a few rare cases, however, the healthy partner remains healthy for many years—most times because of constant restraint of sexual desire. In the rarest of rare cases, the healthy partner doesn't get infected despite lack of sexual restraints—and these humans can only be called miracles of nature."

*****

At the nursing home, as Bishwanath prepared to call it a day, the receptionist confirmed that there were no more patients to be attended to. While she helped Bishwanath, she asked for two days' leave for her cousin's wedding. Barely registering her request, Bishwanath noticed Biplav park his car in the driveway. He made his way to the house when Bishwanath snapped back to reality and asked the receptionist, "How many days will you be gone, and on what dates, specifically?" She mentioned the dates, and Bishwanath approved her leave as he walked out of his cabin.

He headed for the driveway and to the stairway leading to his house.

As soon opened the front door, he overheard Sudha and Biplav engaged in an animated conversation. His curiosity aroused, he entered the house and shut the door noiselessly. He took a few steps to a spot where he could observe them as they continued their conversation in the living room.

An excited Biplav was telling Sudha about how the doctor said that even an HIV- person could marry an HIV+ person, and that meant that he too could marry Aahuti. Sudha asked, "Does Aahuti feel the same way about this marriage?"

He replied, unable to hide the truth from his *bhabhi*, "Aahuti is dead against this marriage, and wants to keep me away from her life because she feels I would be signing my own death certificate if I marry her."

Sudha supported Aahuti's decision to keep herself out of Biplav's life, as she too was not open to the idea of Biplav marrying an HIV+ girl. When Biplav declared his intention to marry Aahuti as final and irrevocable, Sudha tried to talk him out of it. She said, "I sympathise with Aahuti, but I believe she should marry and settle down with an HIV+ man who would understand her better. I'm even willing to look for an HIV+ partner for her."

Biplav defended Aahuti, saying, "She hasn't contracted HIV because of any sexual indiscretion or needle-sharing out of an addiction to drugs. She was injected with contaminated blood, and that could happen to anybody; even to people like us."

Biplav then asked, "What if *dada* had become HIV+ because of blood transfusion? Would you have left him then? Or what if this had happened to you? Would you have expected *dada* to leave you then? Or what if I myself had fallen prey to such an accident? How would I feel if I had found out that all those I loved were quarantining me from their lives? What happened with Aahuti could happen with anybody. Does that mean she should be left alone to die?"

Sudha found herself unable to answer Biplav's questions. Just then, Bishwanath walked into the room and said, "Already being married to someone is entirely different from having an affair. Marriage is an unbreakable bond, and it can withstand whatever accidents or calamities come its way; but that is not the case with something like a mere infatuation."

Taken aback by Bishwanath's sudden appearance, Biplav got flustered. He hesitated for a moment but stood his ground. When he began to speak again, he seemed to have lost his earlier confidence and stammered a little as he said, "*Dada*, I am not merely infatuated with Aahuti. I already consider her as my life partner, and nothing is going to change that."

"Have you even spared a minute to think about what will happen to us?" Bishwanath asked. "How will your *bhabhi* and I cope with our lives, knowing that the Biplav we brought up like a son, and who means everything to us, has chosen death over life for a girl he knows for only few months?!"

Biplav strove hard to make him understand. Calmly, he said, "It's not a matter of months, *dada*. I feel like destiny made her for me, and it seems like I've known her for a long time."

Attempting to get some sense into his brother's head, Bishwanath said, "I like Aahuti too. I think she's a wonderful girl. I'm only against her now because of this disease. I accept that in the past, I thought she was your ideal mate, but now, things have changed. Marrying an HIV+ girl will only mean disease, destruction, and death for you."

Biplav tried to explain, "HIV doesn't mean the end of the world, and people can live a long life if they take their medication regularly."

Bishwanath countered his argument and said, "That's a possibility, but cannot be ascertained. HIV means fear, depression, and despair—not only for the one who is infected with it, but also for everybody around them."

Unable to see his brother's point, Biplav said, "Aahuti will be able to stay in this house and do her regular job without infecting anybody."

An irritated Bishwanath reminded him that he was a doctor and he knew that HIV spreads only through sexual intercourse, or from mother to child apart from blood transfusion and sharing of needles, and that is exactly why he could never agree to their marriage. "Apart from the danger of being infected with HIV, you will also have to face being ostracised from the community that you live in, and will be condemned to living the life of a social outcast. Today, Aahuti's condition is a secret but slowly, people will get to know about it and will begin to distance themselves from her. The society that we live in is very ruthless towards any individual or group that threatens to throw its sense of security off balance. It is going to be a very hard life for her, and if you join her, then it will become the same for you too," Bishwanath warned.

Frustrated by his brother's sermons, Biplav said, "This mindset will have to change. This society will have to accept people like Aahuti in its fold and somebody will have to fight for what is right, just as Raja Ram Mohan Roy once fought for widow remarriage."

His voice laced with anger, Bishwanath taunted, "So you want to lead a revolution now, do you? And pretend to yourself that you are a great revolutionary?"

His taunt riled Biplav up and he exploded with rage, declaring aloud, "I am not a revolutionary, neither am I interested in leading a revolution, nor is my love for Aahuti an act, and I refuse to turn my back to her for fear of anyone or anything—even death."

Bishwanath raised his hand and Biplav was stunned to silence by his slap. Sudha immediately came between the two and held Biplav. "What have you done?!" an aghast Sudha asked Bishwanath.

Bishwanath didn't seem repentant for having slapped Biplav and issued a stern warning to him: "You will NOT let that girl enter this house as your wife. Get that clear in your head."

A defiant Biplav looked at Bishwanath straight in the eye and said to him with an air of finality, "In that case, it would be better that I leave this house forever," and stormed into his room to pack his belongings.

*****

In his moment of need, Biplav turned to Salil for help. He called on his friend, who took him to an empty house nearby. The lock of the door to a one-room furnished apartment clicked, and Salil entered with Biplav, carrying a large suitcase and 2-3 large bags. The walls of the apartment were filled with beautiful paintings—mostly depicting sorrow and loneliness. The man who owned this apartment—Salil's uncle—was a really good painter, and after his wife's death, he shut himself up in this room for many years and kept painting to live beyond the memory of his beloved wife. Then, about 8 months ago, he went to

London and started a restaurant there, never to return. He left the keys of this house with Salil, and asked him to look after the house.

Biplav looked around as they placed the luggage on the floor. Salil opened the door to a spacious balcony and showed Biplav the huge *pandal* coming up for the Durga *puja* in the open ground there.

Meanwhile, Biplav was unable to tear himself away from the paintings. He was very impressed with them and commented to Salil, "Your *mausa* (uncle) must have really loved his wife."

Salil agreed, but added, "Your love for Aahuti is no less if you are so unwilling to let go of her hand, even in a situation like this."

Salil suddenly hugged Biplav and told him he would always be there for him. As soon as Salil left, Biplav began to unpack his things, but soon his attention was drawn back to the paintings. He moved from one painting to another, feeling deeply affected by them as his eyes brimmed with tears.

*****

Something woke Bishwanath late in the night, and he found Sudha missing from the bed. He switched on the light and looked around, but she was nowhere to be seen. Puzzled, he got out of bed and walked out of his bedroom. He noticed the light on in Biplav's room, and as he walked towards it he began to hear the faint sound of Sudha weeping. Entering Biplav's room, he found Sudha on Biplav's bed, crying. He went to her and held her, as she turned to him and sobbed, "Bring him back. Bring my Biplav back to me!"

Bishwanath consoled her and calmed her down. He then said, "If we both agree with Biplav's decision to marry Aahuti, then this will all be over. At least this way we can expect his conscience to wake up some day and tell him that he is doing a great wrong to himself and to us by his way of thinking. We have to make him realise that he is not doing the right thing, and this way, at least there is a chance of him changing his mind."

*****

The next day, Dr. Chugani studied Aahuti's test reports showing her CD4 count, viral load, and other important information. Biplav asked him, "Doctor, how do family members generally react to somebody who has been diagnosed with HIV?"

Dr. Chugani said, "I have found that people from lower and uneducated classes tend to be more accepting and tolerant when somebody in their family is diagnosed with HIV. I meet most of these patients during my biweekly hours at the hospital, since almost all of them are from lower middle class and lower class, and aren't very educated. I find that people who are from the middle class and upper class and are better educated are the ones who are less tolerant if a member of their family becomes HIV+ for any reason—be it drugs, blood transfusion, or sexual contact." He added, "A strange situation, considering that education and a better standard of living are supposed to make one more understanding and tolerant. HIV is just a disease, but the social stigma, ignorance, and misunderstandings attached to it are the real curse, and that is what proves to be more deadly to the patient than the virus itself."

Thanking the doctor for his help, Biplav and Aahuti left the clinic. On his way out, they were unknowingly spotted by Prasenjit Dutta, who became suspicious and hid himself so as to not let them spot him. As soon as they were gone, he rushed into the clinic to meet Dr. Chugani.

Under normal circumstances, a doctor would never reveal personal information about his patients to a stranger, especially HIV related information. But Rtd. Col. Prasenjit Dutta, in his own inimitable style, managed to convince Dr. Chugani to spill the beans and managed to get the truth about Aahuti out of the cornered Doctor. As expected, he was stunned on learning about her HIV+ status.

Prasenjit rushed to the Sanjivani Institute, where a large *pandal* for the upcoming *puja* was under construction. He parked his car, stepped out, gave the workers some instructions and proceeded towards the building to find Biplav, who was busy teaching accountancy to 5-7 kids in a classroom. He interrupted the class and asked Biplav to step outside for a word. He told him, "I have just returned from Dr. Chugani's clinic, and I now know everything there is to know about Aahuti's little secret." Biplav was taken aback with the way Prasenjit confronted him directly. When he tried to speak, no words came out of his mouth, seemingly stuck in his throat. His lips quivered, and his face twitched. Prasenjit could clearly see the pain inside him and protectively put his arm around Biplav. "Come with me," he said, "we will talk."

Prasenjit took Biplav to his house, where Biplav sat across Prasenjit on the sofa, sipping from his glass of whiskey. In a few swift moves, Biplav finished his drink, and Prasenjit proceeded to make him another, while whipping up another glass for himself as well. Now, after having downed a few drinks, Biplav was unable to stop the tears from coming. He'd never felt sadder in his life. 'Why did it have to happen like this? I don't feel like going on with my life anymore,' he thought to himself.

He looked up to find Prasenjit staring at him with bloodshot eyes. "Stop feeling sorry for yourself and for her," Prasenjit thundered, "Bengal doesn't need another Devdas. Bengal needs men like lions who can forge their own destinies with an iron will. Man up!" Quoting Verse 3 from Chapter 2 of the Bhagwad Gita, Prasenjit challenged him, "Get up on your feet."

An excited Biplav stood up and shouted, "I am not afraid of death, or HIV/AIDS. It is only Aahuti who is stopping me."

"Are you telling me she is stronger than you if she is able to stop you successfully?" Prasenjit taunted him and began to laugh. Biplav got furious at Prasenjit and began to yell at him: "*You* tell me, what should I do? Tell me!"

Prasenjit shot back, "Why should I tell you what to do? It is you who has to decide what you have to do. Just remember one thing—'everything is fair in love and war'."

Close to tears once again, Biplav said slowly, "I don't want to force her. I don't want to hurt her."

Unable to deal with Biplav's self-loathing, Prasenjit lamented, "Hurt her?! Love means hurt, love means pain… love means togetherness at any cost!" He continued, "Once upon a time, I was at the same crossroads that you are now, and I did not dare cross the limits imposed upon me by the world I lived in, and turned back. To this day, I regret my decision and wish I had the guts when I needed it."

Biplav couldn't hold back a snigger. He said, "It is easier to preach to others, isn't it?"

Stung by Biplav's taunt, Prasenjit suddenly leapt to his feet and rushed to him, grabbing his collar. With silent fury, he said, "I am not preaching to you, I am preaching to myself, you idiot." He roared, "You are my past and I am your future." He continued to scream at Biplav, and shaking with anger he said, "Look at me, you idiot. Do you want to grow old like me, alone and repentant for what I never dared to do?"

In the distance outside, the faint music from the Durga *puja* could be heard as Biplav stood before Prasenjit, shaken to his core. He thought for a few moments and then suddenly calmed down, as though he had reached a decision. "No," he said, with quiet determination.

He then headed to Rabindra Sarobar, where he asked Aahuti to meet him. As soon as she arrived, he got to work with trying to convince her to marry him. She refused and said with anger, "Why have you brought up this topic again when I specifically asked you not to do so?"

Biplav argued, "I am responsible for your HIV status anyway. *I* fired the bullet that wounded you. *I* took you to *dada* instead of taking you to the police. *I* brought the contaminated blood from the blood bank. If you are HIV+ today, it is only because of me. You need to give me a chance for redemption by marrying me."

She shouted back, "I have no interest in becoming an instrument for *your* redemption, nor do I want your pity. Whatever happened was just an accident—rather, a chain of accidents. It was my fate, and I must bear it alone. Either you accept me as nothing more than a friend, or I will never meet you again."

Biplav gave up; he was tired of fighting. Softly, he asked, "Tell me one last thing—would you have married me if I too was HIV+?"

His question shocked Aahuti and she snapped, "What on earth do you mean by that?" Biplav didn't reply, letting his expression speak for itself as he looked on.

*****

Without another thought as to what he could do, the only way out for Biplav seemed to be deceit. He called Salil and asked him to procure a medicine for him that would help convince Aahuti to change her mind. Salil went to a clinic nearby, where a medical technician prepared a clear liquid, pouring a few millilitres into a very small glass container with a dropper, put a cap on it and handed it to Salil, who thanked him for this favour. The man warned him, "If you get caught by the Police with this, it should not lead them back to me. I meant it." Salil reassured him and promised that it wouldn't as he ran out to meet Biplav.

Since they couldn't risk meeting in a populated spot, Biplav told Salil to meet him at the Hatibagan *pandal*. Approaching a very determined looking Biplav there, Salil gave him the little bottle and warned him not to use more than 3-4 drops, else it could result in coma, hospitalisation, or even death.

"The medicine will begin to take effect in 20 minutes and will last for 4-5 hours, he said. Hesitantly, he asked, "You're fully aware of the consequences of your actions, aren't you?" Biplav nodded slowly as he walked away.

*****

Back in her room, Aahuti put the final touches to her makeup, looking resplendent in her new *sari*. Like all Bengalis, especially Bengali girls, she too had dressed up in her finest for the *Puja* evening. Jyotirmoi came in, dressed to go out for the evening, and told Aahuti that Biplav and his friends had come to pick her up, and turned to leave the room. Aahuti, who had been expecting Biplav, took a final look at herself in the mirror before making her way out.

She entered the living room, where Biplav was waiting for her with Salil, his girlfriend Krutika, and Krutika's cousin Sreshtha. They were all busy feasting on the sweets Dolly had served them. Dolly and Arijit were also ready to go out. Biplav looked up as Aahuti walked towards them, dazzled by her form. He had never seen Aahuti look so beautiful. He introduced her to his friends and soon, they all stood up to leave. Biplav invited Dolly and Arijit to join them, but the parents refused, saying, "Now come on. What are we oldies going to do with you youngsters?"

"When we were young, we hardly ever came back home before sunrise," Dolly reminisced. "Now hurry up and head on over to the Sanjivani Institute. Colonel *Saheb* has invited you to his *pandal*," she said.

Biplav said, "My *dada* and *bhabhi* are also headed there."

Dolly said, "This is the first time Aahuti is not going out with her old school friends, but with a completely new set of friends! I hope they all have a great time. Jyotirmoi, would you like to go with them?" Jyotirmoi shook his head, as he was going out with his classmates.

The troupe was finally on their way. They arrived at the Sanjivani Institute, where a supercharged Prasenjit was dancing before the idol on the *pandal* during the *Puja*. The city had come to life that night—everywhere one turned, there were idols of the Goddess, the unbelievable crowd thronging the many *pandals*, the ecstatic and noisy celebrations, beautifully outfitted families and friends meeting, eating out... there was joy everywhere.

Aahuti, Biplav, and their gang went from one place to another amidst all this and enjoyed every moment. At one *pandal*, Biplav and Salil got the *khichdi prasad* for everyone in individual plates, and Biplav spiked one plate with the liquid from the little bottle. He gave that particular plate to Aahuti. They kept roaming around and soon, Aahuti began to feel giddy and had to support herself on pillars and parked vehicles. She told Biplav she wasn't feeling very well and wished to rest her head somewhere. Biplav put his arm around her for support and soon, she clung to him. "You'll be alright soon. Maybe the crowd is making you feel suffocated," he said as he patted her affectionately.

Soon, Aahuti began to feel worse, and Biplav suggested they go to the Colonel *Saheb's* place for a while, since it was close by and Biplav had the keys. "Colonel Saheb must be busy at the *pandal*, but I'm sure he won't mind," he said. The truth was that Biplav was taking her to the apartment Salil had arranged for him to stay at. They left the others and promised to join them once she felt better. Biplav moved through the crowd with Aahuti under his arm. She fell just as they were reaching the apartment, and Biplav put his arm around her waist to keep her up. She began giggling and enjoyed Biplav being so close to her, laughing and joking with him, the effects of the drug in her system acting very much like alcohol.

They got to the apartment, where the din of the *puja* celebrations seemed too loud because of the pandal right outside. Biplav locked the door and immediately pulled the almost limp Aahuti in his arms, holding her tight against his body. "What is happening to me, Biplav?" She asked.

Biplav didn't reply, but just kept looking into her eyes. "Do you love me?" he asked.

"Yes," she said, unable to hold back her true feelings, "I love you more than anything."

"Then why have you not been allowing me to come close to you?" He said.

"I think of you all the time—I dream of you every night, and every morning the first thought I have on waking up are thoughts about you," she confessed.

"Will you be mine forever?" he asked.

She blushed and nodded and then laid her head on his chest. With one finger under her chin, he lifted her face to him and kissed her. Unable to resist him any longer, she wrapped her arms around his neck and kissed him back passionately.

Almost instantly, however, she began resisting him and pushed him away. She remembered that she could never enter into any physical relations with him. She suddenly became suspicious that she had been drugged by him, and he had planned this whole thing out. She asked "Are my suspicions true? Have you drugged me so you could have your way with me?"

Biplav said nothing, and continued to look at her. She asked again, her speech slurring. He nodded. "Why would you do that?!" she asked him, but she couldn't hold her body up any longer and fell into his arms again.

"I did it because I love you more than I love myself, and I cannot bear to live my life without you," Biplav said as he picked her up and carried her to the bed.

She protested feebly but was unable to resist him anymore. He laid her on the bed and took off his shirt. As he began to undress her, slowly unwrapping her *sari*, her reluctance faded away and she too became a willing participant. Soon, they were clasped in each other's arms and made passionate love with no restraints.

The next morning, the sun's rays filtered through the curtains to where Biplav and Aahuti lay asleep on the bed, their half-naked bodies intertwined in a passionate embrace. Aahuti's eyes suddenly jerked open and she looked around, trying to figure out where she was when she realised that Biplav was spooning her, fast sleep. Unwilling to accept the situation she found herself in, she let out a loud gasp, which woke Biplav from his deep slumber. She tried to free herself from his arms and got off the bed. Instantly taking note of her partially naked state, she fumbled around for her *sari*, which lay in a heap by the foot of the bed. She grabbed the end and began to wrap it around herself, covering her dignity.

Breathing hard, she stood there motionless as she grew more aware of her body. Biplav sat up and looked at her, waiting for her to say something. She glanced in his direction but immediately lowered her gaze. It was then that she noticed the patches of blood on the bed sheet and it hit her hard— she had sex with Biplav last night. She felt the dried blood with her hands and looked at Biplav. Her eyes filled with tears and soon began to flow down her cheeks as her whole body trembled. "Why did you do this?" She asked between sobs.

Biplav caressed her affectionately and wiped away her tears. "It was necessary, that's why," he answered calmly. "Now there are no more obstacles between us," he justified himself.

She refused to accept this and began to lament and cry out loud as she repeatedly hit Biplav all over. Biplav let her keep going. She soon tired out, fell silent and collapsed into his arms. He held her protectively and she sank onto him. She slowly gave in and began to return his affection as it dawned on her that Biplav had done the right thing. She willingly snuggled into him and began to kiss his chest, shoulders, arms, and neck, finally trailing back to his lips, leaving him with a passionate kiss.

The couple headed for Dr. Chugani's clinic for the routine consultation, where the doctor was shocked to know about what happened between the two of them. Aahuti asked Dr. Chugani, "Do you think Biplav is HIV+ as well now?"

The doctor responded flatly, "Most likely, but we can't be 100% certain. The tests will start showing the presence of antibodies only after a minimum of six weeks once the blood has been infected."

Aahuti wanted to know, in as clear terms as possible, if it took only a single occasion of unprotected sex to get Biplav HIV+. Dr. Chugani hesitated as he looked into Biplav's eyes. Biplav secretly signalled to him to say yes. Questioning his ethics, Dr. Chugani stopped to think for a minute before he said, "Yes. We can be sure that Biplav too is now HIV+."

Aahuti felt defeated and her last hopes seemed to have been crushed. Dr. Chugani told her, Look, at the bright side of this situation. Thank *Maa Durga* for blessing you with a man who will love you till his last breath, and you should go ahead and marry him. One cannot say if a permanent cure for HIV will be developed in the near future, but I am hopeful. After all, many top doctors are trying to find the miracle drug to cure it. Why stop living life and loving in the meantime?" Aahuti saw the truth in the doctor's words. She turned to Biplav, took his hand, and kissed it.

Biplav then took Aahuti home from the clinic, where he asked her parents to fix the date for their wedding. He also asked them not to consult his elder brother for any details, as he had turned against this marriage. Biplav lied to them and said, "The daughter of one of *dada's* wealthy friends has just returned from London after finishing her MD. *Dada* wants me to marry her so that she too can run and expand his nursing home, while also bringing in a lot of dowry."

Aahuti's parents were shocked at Bishwanath changing his colours. Arijit applauded Biplav's decision to rebel and offered to let him become his *ghar jamai* (live-in son-in-law) after marriage. "This house has enough space and privacy for the two of you," he added.

Biplav appreciated his offer, but felt that they'd prefer to live in his one-room apartment for some time after marriage before making the move after a couple of months. Arijit liked this idea and felt that this *puja* had truly blessed him. Since it was the occasion of *Navami*, Dolly decided that they should celebrate, and so, the family headed out to wine and dine joyfully.

*****

Arrangements were being made and celebrations were on to take the *Durga* idol out for the immersion. Busy with all the action, Prasenjit took a break to talk to Biplav. He was worried that the news that Biplav—who had cheated his former employer, besides also committing the act of forgery, crimes for which he spent a year in jail—was negatively affecting the image of his NGO. Biplav offered to quit, but Prasenjit had another plan up his sleeve. He said to Biplav, "An old friend is about to show up to meet me." As Biplav wondered about the identity of this mystery friend, Prasenjit pointed to Mukhtar entering the gates of the Sanjivani Institute, waving to them.

*****

The processions for the immersion of the *Durga* idols were crowding and choking the roads as people bid a very emotional farewell to the Goddess. Many of them were dancing to the beats of the drums of all kinds. Among them was a familiar face—Chintan Ghosh. A man observed him carefully from a distance and then made a call to somebody. He muttered a few things into the phone, all the while not taking his eyes off Chintan, as the crowds marched on.

During this time, Prasenjit, Biplav, Mukhtar and many others, including the kids from the Sanjivani Institute, immersed their *Durga* idol in the Hoogli river with the Vidyasagar Setu standing tall behind them. After their immersion ritual was over, the three men quietly slipped away and mingled with the crowd, their eyes searching for somebody. Soon, Biplav spotted Chintan in the distance with a group of people taking their idol into the water. He asked the other two to come with him and they all swam in the water towards Chintan. They reached Chintan just as he and his mates were immersing their idol in the river. Prasenjit, Biplav, and Mukhtar got close to Chintan and as the idol toppled over into the water, the trio managed to drown Chintan beneath the idol. Chintan began to thrash about in the water as he sank deeper with the Goddess figurine.

Not a single person from his group noticed what was happening and they were all oblivious to Chintan's plight. The three men dragged him away while forcibly keeping him underwater as he flayed about. They swam far away from the crowd and after a couple of minutes, Chintan's body went limp. They pulled him up close to a boat, which seemed as though it was waiting just for them. The lone boatman was accompanied by a man who was known to Prasenjit. He was the same man who had kept a watch on Chintan during the *visarjan* procession.

They dragged Chintan into the boat and the boatman rowed away. Prasenjit resuscitated Chintan who coughed roughly as he regained consciousness. "By the time your friends notice that you're missing, you will have vanished," Prasenjit informed him, "and they will begin to look for your dead body, thinking that you've drowned in the river, just like the many others who drown during *visarjan* every year." When he saw Biplav approaching them, the expression on Chintan's face began to change and his body quivered with fear.

The group took Chintan to a secluded village nearby, where they tied him to a wooden chair. There seemed to be some kind of small animal thrashing around wildly inside a small pot kept in a corner, making a terrifying sound. Shivering with fear, Chintan wept and pleaded for mercy as his attention was constantly drawn towards the pot.

"Are you really a Bengali?" Prasenjit asked him.

"Yes, yes. I am a Bengali just like you, and I too am a devotee of Durga *Ma*."

Prasenjit then said, "In that case, I'm quite certain then like all Bengalis, you too must have pictures of Ramkrishna Paramhamsa, Swami Vivekananda, and Rabindranath Tagore in your house."

"Yes! Yes! Their photographs are hung on the walls at home, and I just adore and worship them. I've even heard my mother sing the Rabindra *sangeet* since I was a child," Chintan reminisced as he spoke the truth about himself.

"So was it their ghosts that inspired you to stab another Bengali in the back?!" Prasenjit screamed, "And that too commit such an act against this man here –" he pointed at Biplav "– who is a true and rare gem among the youth of Bengal today."

Prasenjit asked Mukhtar to bring out the murder weapon and finish off this good for nothing fellow. Mukhtar went to the pot and brought out a small fish, no longer than a foot. With some effort, he held the wildly thrashing fish in his firm grasp. Prasenjit said to Chintan, "This is the famous *koy*[1] fish, which has been used as a murder weapon since ancient times in Bengal. This fish doesn't die easily; even if it is cut into many small pieces. When it is thrust inside the mouth of a man, it will go into his belly and tear him apart, inside out. Once the fish has done its job, we will throw your body in the river and everybody will think you were probably eaten up by the fish during the immersion." Prasenjit asked Chintan as Mukhtar held the fish close to his face, "Do you want to die such a horrible death?"

Chintan was practically paralysed with fear and he whimpered, "Please, spare me. I don't want to die yet."

Prasenjit's voice grew louder as he hollered, "Wimps like you are a disgrace to us Bengalis. By betraying a Bengali, you've betrayed our culture and all of us. For what?! Just for the money that Saurabh Dalmiya threw at you, like one throws a bone to a dog? Has it become *so* easy to buy a Bengali's integrity?"

Chintan began to weep: "I didn't like what Saurabh did to Biplav, but he convinced me to take his side, and I was

---

[1] A species of fish used by dacoits in the 17th and 18th century

greedy for the money." He begged for forgiveness and promised, "I will do whatever it takes for Biplav to have his name cleared. What I did was wrong and I myself have been mad at Saurabh or anyone who has insulted the Bengali pride and honour. Unfortunately, I was never brave enough to retaliate because I considered myself to be weak and poor."

"Weak in your own home?!" Prasenjit challenged him, "Even a mouse feels like a lion inside his own hole, and you being a son of this very land feel weak here?" Prasenjit whacked Mukhtar's wrist, forcing him to drop the fish on the ground. It began to flail violently and jump about all over. "Look at that small fish," Prasenjit pointed, "it is so strong and full of fight, even though it is so small and out of water. And look at you—an adult man, feeling weak and ineffectual in your own home."

Prasenjit's words struck a chord with Chintan and he stopped crying right away. He looked Prasenjit right in the eye and said, "You're right. If all Bengalis rid themselves of their petty minds and stood by each other, no outsider could ever dare to dominate us in our own home." He turned to Biplav and asked for his forgiveness. He said, "I swear I'll tell you everything about what happened in Macau before a magistrate."

Prasenjit interrupted, "If you do that, then you'll go to jail as well—for being an accomplice. Are you ready for that?"

"Yes, I am," said a proud Chintan, "I will not let people like Saurabh trample our Bengali pride under their feet anymore."

His feelings towards Chintan changing with every word, Prasenjit said softly, "In that case, I will see to it that you are produced in the court as the public prosecutor's prime witness, and that you are exempted from any sentence." With this, the group let Chintan go.

Soon after, Chintan's statement was published in newspapers across the state, and Chintan surrendered himself to the police. The television news channels picked up the story from there and soon it felt like the whole city had begun demanding action against Saurabh Dalmiya. Finally, Saurabh was arrested and sent to a lock-up, while a charge sheet was filed against him. All the action was caught live on camera for news channels. A news reporter asked Koel about her reaction to all this and she burst out against Saurabh, screaming, "He cheated not only Biplav, but me as well. If the charges against him are true, then I will file for divorce right away."

Huddled before the television in their living room, Bishwanath and Sudha were watching all this on TV when the doorbell rang. Sudha opened the door and was pleasantly surprised to find Biplav standing there with Prasenjit. Prasenjit dragged Biplav inside to meet his *dada* and *bhabhi* to celebrate the occasion. Bishwanath was happy that Saurabh was finally getting punished for his deeds and that Biplav's innocence was out in the open for everyone to see.

Prasenjit tried to patch things up between the two brothers, and requested Bishwanath and Sudha to be present at Biplav's wedding with Aahuti, which had been fixed for the following week. "So this is the real reason why you came here," Bishwanath's eyes flashed in sudden anger. He burst into a fit of rage and accused Prasenjit of turning Biplav's head and playing mentor to him. "It is only because you pretend to be his Godfather that Biplav has become a rebel," Bishwanath screamed. Prasenjit tried to explain things calmly to Bishwanath, but Bishwanath walked off into his bedroom, asking Sudha to bid goodbye to the two gentlemen.

As Bishwanath shut the door to his bedroom, Sudha quietly said, "Be patient with *dada*. He will accept Aahuti in due time." She kissed Biplav's forehead and blessed him.

Biplav asked, "*Bhabhi*, will you at least be there for my wedding?"

Unable to look him in the eye, she said, "I'll try my best." Biplav then asked, "Are you also angry with me?" Sudha shook her head and told him that she wished every girl would be able to find as loving and committed a man as Biplav as her life partner. Feeling ecstatic at hearing these words, Biplav hugged her and left.

*****

The week went by in the blink of an eye and before they knew it, Aahuti and Biplav's wedding day had arrived. Arijit's house was lavishly decorated for their marriage, and their ceremony was conducted in typical Bengali tradition. Besides the other guests the Senguptas had invited, Sudha was present along with Prasenjit, Salil, Krutika, Jhantu, and Dr. Chugani. The newlywed couple received blessings and gifts from everybody. As a wedding present, Prasenjit gave them an all expenses paid stay for two weeks in a hotel in

Darjeeling for their honeymoon, which the happy couple accepted with great joy.

Aahuti and Biplav were soon off on their honeymoon, as they rode the train up the hills of Darjeeling. They spent a few days in absolute bliss, until one day, when Aahuti found herself in a strange predicament—she had a strong hunch that she was probably pregnant. She touched her belly and stared hard at her reflection in the mirror, questioning the fate of a child born to an HIV+ mother. She came out of the bathroom and rushed to Biplav and said, "I-I don't know how, but I have a strong feeling I'm pregnant. I just threw up." Biplav wondered how this happened so quickly, as they had been married for only 12 days. She then remembered the night that they indulged in lovemaking before marriage. It seemed as though their first time had got her pregnant.

Biplav smiled and kissed her. "Our love has bore fruit," he said. She didn't share his enthusiasm, and wondered if she should get an abortion done. Biplav was taken aback at the mere mention of an abortion, not understanding her fear that she may have transmitted her disease to a life that had only just begun.

They cut short their honeymoon to rush back home. The very next day after they got back, the worried husband and wife headed for Dr. Chugani's clinic to know the fate of their unborn child. They met with him and asked him several questions about the risks involved. Dr. Chugani explained everything there was to know about pregnancy and childbirth for an HIV+ couple. He said, "Under medical supervision, there are more than 70-90% chances of the baby being born healthy."

Aahuti, who was at her wit's end, asked frantically, "But what if my baby is among the unlucky 10-30%?" Letting out an audible sigh, Dr. Chugani said, "That, unfortunately, is a risk you will have to be willing to take."

Aahuti decided that she didn't want to take that risk. "It would amount to gambling with the life of my newborn baby. If all goes well and the baby is born HIV-, then everything will be fine and everyone will love the baby. But if it is born HIV+, then life will become like a death sentence for it, and I will be the one responsible for bringing such an unlucky soul into this world." With a firm voice, she said, "I've decided that I want an abortion. If I wish to have children, I'll adopt one in the future."

Biplav, however, was against the abortion and wanted her to have the baby. "I want to take the risk of having an HIV+ child on our conscience. Even daily life is full of risks, but we continu to survive, one day at a time, hoping for the best. If we fear the worst in every situation, then it will soon become impossible to even step out of the house for fear of an accident. Even staying at home could pose certain threats—we could get electrocuted, burn due to a short circuit... the possibilities are endless." Striving to get his wife to understand his perspective, he said, "On the other hand, think of how meaningful our lives will become if we have a healthy baby." Dr. Chugani agreed with Biplav, and Aahuti reluctantly gave in to Biplav.

Dr. Chugani gave a prescription of the medicines Aahuti needed as her CD4 count was nearing 500, and instructed her that once she started with the medication, she could not risk missing her dose even for a single day under any circumstances. "Henceforth, you will also have to consult an obstetrician/ gynaecologist, so as to monitor the development of your baby. You can meet with Dr. Aruna Broota. She's an excellent doctor at the Apollo Gleaneagles Hospital who has handled such cases before." Aahuti and Biplav gathered their belongings—the prescriptions and doctor's information in tow—and left for their journey back home.

That night, Biplav and Aahuti lay in bed, talking. Aahuti was still not entirely certain she wanted to go ahead with her pregnancy. Biplav tried his best to calm her down. "It would be a wonderful thing to play with our child, wouldn't it?" he asked.

"*If* the child is healthy," answered Aahuti, "If the child is born with HIV, then I won't be able to look it in the eye."

Holding her tenderly, Biplav said with confidence, "Everything will be fine. I have faith in our love."

*****

Biplav was teaching a class full of teenagers when Nitin Shah, a man in his 50s, stood by the door with Prasenjit and observed Biplav. He was satisfied with Biplav's teaching methods, and turned to Prasenjit to say, "This boy can make lakhs of rupees every month by teaching at my CA coaching institute." Happy to see that his plan was bearing fruit, Prasenjit smiled loftily at Biplav, completely unaware that fate was trying to make his life better in more ways than one.

Back in his office, Prasenjit conferred with Nitin Shah and Biplav, when the former offered Biplav a good package to teach at his CA coaching institute. Biplav wanted to take it, but he didn't want to quit teaching at the Sanjivani Institute.

"Very well then," counselled Nitin Shah, "you can teach at both places if you wish to."

Prasenjit added, "It will mean, however, that you will have to work extra hard."

Determined to take on the responsibility, Biplav answered, "I am. I'm ready for this."

Nitin Shah patted Biplav's back encouragingly and said, "Now that you're going to be a father soon, I urge you to prepare yourself to work harder to fulfil the new responsibilities coming your way."

*****

During his consultation with Biplav about his HIV test report, Dr. Chugani said "I do hope Aahuti is taking her medicines regularly."

Biplav said that he made sure she did so in his presence. "If I'm not home, I call her when it is time for her to take them, and wait on the line until she's done so," Biplav said.

Dr. Chugani showed Biplav his HIV test report, informing him that he was still testing as HIV-. Biplav was surprised at his being HIV-; even after 4 months of his relationship with Aahuti. Dr. Chugani explained. "Please understand that it is not necessary that an individual is infected with the virus after having unprotected sex only once or twice with an HIV+ person. It may take longer—months, sometimes even years."

Biplav thought hard for a few moments and then asked the doctor not to reveal his HIV- status to anybody. Dr. Chugani understood what he meant, but also warned him, saying, "If you continue like this, then you will definitely contract HIV very soon." Biplav smiled as he put the test report in his pocket and said, "*Jab okhli mein sarr de diya, toh moosalon se kya darna?*"

Biplav left the clinic and headed to a pharmacy nearby to buy the necessary medicines for Aahuti, who was now about 3 months pregnant. He got home and as they settled down, he said, "My CD4 count is still healthy, and while yours is just over 450, the doctor has warned that during pregnancy, you may become prey to one or the other opportunistic infections or diseases, and you have to be very careful."

Aahuti was very disturbed and worried. "What if my worst fear comes true? What if the baby born to me turns out to be HIV+?" She wondered out loud, her voice growing shrill with each question.

Biplav tried to distract her from her pessimistic thoughts, but Aahuti kept coming back full circle. She asked Biplav again, "What will you do if our child is born HIV+?"

Biplav really had no answer to this, except for his belief that their child would be born healthy. He was annoyed with Aahuti for thinking such negative thoughts. He stomped about their room as he took off his clothes, grabbed his towel and headed for a shower to soothe his nerves.

Biplav finished with his shower and dried himself off. As he stepped out of the bathroom with the towel wrapped around his waist, he was shocked to find a fully dressed

Aahuti waiting by the door with her suitcases, an expression of absolute rage blanketing her face. With a puzzled look, he asked, "What's the matter?"

Aahuti replied curtly, "I'm leaving you forever. The first thing I'm going to do is get an abortion, and right after that, I'm filing for divorce."

Biplav rushed to her and shook her by the shoulders, "Have you gone mad, Aahuti?" He stepped away when she suddenly lifted a hand to reveal Biplav's HIV test report. One look at the paper in her hand and Biplav realised that his lies had been uncovered.

She continued glaring at him as her temper rose, making her body tremble. She hissed, "This report very clearly states that you are still HIV-. Yet, you continued to lie to me for the last four months that just like me, you too were HIV+! How dare you?!"

Biplav was stunned into silence by her confrontational attitude. She continued, "Dr. Chugani also lied to me, telling me that it only takes one sexual encounter to pass on the virus to another person. If that were truly the case, then are you trying to tell me that this report is lying? Answer me, Biplav! Tell me—is this report a lie?"

Trying to turn the tables on her, Biplav asked accusatorily, "You searched my pockets when I went for a shower, didn't you?"

Snapping at his audacity, Aahuti screamed, "Don't you dare try to change the subject. Tell me the truth—is this report doctored? Is it fake?"

Biplav stood silently, rooted to his spot. Aahuti screamed again, "Why don't you say anything? Answer me—is this report fake?!"

Biplav shook his head slowly.

Aahuti sneered, "Then why did you tell me that your CD4 count was normal some time ago? How dare you think you can just lie to me like this?"

Biplav didn't say a word.

"You ordered Dr. Chugani to lie to me, didn't you?" she lamented. Once again, Biplav didn't reply, but his body language made it clear that he accepted his manipulation of Dr. Chugani.

"What do you think of yourself?" Aahuti scoffed.

"If I was actually thinking about myself, then I'd figure a few things out about my own head. I have thought of nothing else but you ever since I got to know of your illness, because by then, you'd managed to make a place for yourself in my heart. But your stubbornness forced you to keep me at bay, which was impossible for me. I didn't want to cause you any pain because I loved you and still love you with all my heart, and will continue to do so till my last breath." He approached her slowly as he said, "That's why I was forced to lie to you. Forgive me, Aahuti. I'm willing to accept whatever punishment you have for me. Just know that I can't live without you."

Aahuti, who stood silently as Biplav spoke, finally said, "Did you not stop to think for one second what I was going through when I thought I had infected you as well? Did you not take my guilt into consideration? And now, we're going to have a baby who could probably be…" She broke down before she could complete her statement.

Just then, the doorbell rang. Aahuti opened the door to find a bewildered Arijit and Dolly standing before her. They both came in and realised what they'd walked into as they spotted Aahuti's suitcase in the doorway. Surprised by their arrival, Biplav asked, "What brought you here at this hour?"

Arijit replied, "We received a call from Aahuti, asking us to get her as soon as we could. What's the matter? Have you two fought?"

Aahuti proceeded to tell her parents everything. As expected, they were shocked to learn the truth. Biplav accepted that he had been lying to her and had convinced Dr. Chugani to lie to her as well. He knew that if she came to know of the truth, she would distance herself from him once again. Aahuti's anger rose again and she shrieked, "You cheated me!"

Biplav told her, "Aahuti, I really don't care if I am HIV+ or HIV-. All I care about is you, and I will do what it takes to keep you in my life. I'm certain that my test results will start showing HIV+ sooner or later, but it doesn't matter much to me as it will no longer be a barrier between us."

Arijit and Dolly were still stunned by the news of their daughter's terminal disease when they finally realised that Biplav married an HIV+ girl out of choice—out of love for her. They applauded his heroism and calmed Aahuti down, convincing her that Biplav was forced to lie and cheat because he loved her. Aahuti broke down once again and cried her heart out as she hugged Biplav. Dolly soothed her and decided that it would be best if the both moved in to their house, to which Biplav agreed.

Chapter 5

February 2015

The yellow star slowly emerged from the dark underworld, signalling the birth of a new day. Sudha's face glowed with excitement as she called up Bishwanath to give him the good news—a healthy and normal son was born to Biplav and Aahuti. Bishwanath, ecstatic to hear this news, hurried to the hospital with Jhantu, where he was delighted to see Biplav's son in Aahuti's loving arms. Even Prasenjit Dutta was there as everybody celebrated the birth of an HIV-child. Dr. Chugani and Dr. Aruna were congratulated and thanked by the family.

Biplav stood in a corner of the room, still cross with Bishwanath, and objected to his being there. Shattered by his brother's feelings for him, a deflated Bishwanath was about to leave when Sudha intervened and decided that it was time to reveal to everybody the sacrifice that Bishwanath made for Biplav. "Bishwanath and Biplav's parents died in a plane crash when Biplav was just 4 years old, and Bishwanath was engaged to marry me. However, because Bishwanath feared that we would end up neglecting Biplav if we had children of our own, Bishwanath presented me with one condition for marriage—that we would not have kids of our own. When I agreed, Bishwanath went ahead and got a vasectomy to ensure that he didn't have any children of his own." She stopped to catch her breath. Holding back tears, she continued, "Bishwanath and I brought up Biplav as our one and only son, so it was very natural for him to react to Biplav the way he did for marrying an HIV+ Aahuti."

Realising now the extent of his *dada's* love for him, Biplav fell at Bishwanath's feet, asking for his forgiveness for having hurt him.

Bishwanath made him stand up and hugged him. He said, "I am so proud of you for having stood by Aahuti through all this." He placed his hand on Aahuti's head and blessed her with a long and fulfilling life. He said to her, "Life mustn't be long; it must be big and grand. It must be a celebration!"

Everybody was beaming with happiness as Biplav picked up his son and handed him over to Bishwanath and asked him to name the little boy. Staring intently at the little angel's face, Bishwanath named him Bibhuti—one who would grow up to earn great name and fame.

The End

Acknowledgements

My thanks to the almighty, for providing me with the opportunity to publish my first book. Though I have written many more stories, which are unpublished as of now, this first book will always remain closest to my heart. I have worked hard to bring this story to life, and have tried my best to ensure it lives up to its expectations. As the story revolves around love in the times of hardship, and discusses the sensitive issue of HIV/AIDS, it required lot of intensive research in order to acquire the facts.

I would like to acknowledge all those who have made this journey possible for me.

I am grateful to all the Chartered Accountants who provided me with the basic information about their field. My thanks to the doctors who guided me and helped me understand the psychological and physical state of the patients suffering from this evil disease. Due to some professional restrictions, I am unable to disclose their names here, but I hope they read this story and take note of their contributions.

I am blessed that my second profession, i.e., Astro Consultancy, has supported me along the way, and has helped me stand on my own two feet and live my life on my own terms.

My everlasting gratitude to my wife, Shaloo. Her valuable inputs helped me maintain the essence of the story and the glory of all the characters. We both share the same affection with the story, and hold it very close to our hearts. She was my relentless first critic and persistently provided me with valuable inputs as the story progressed. She was a continuous source of motivation and support, and her feedback helped me shape my characters with more finesse.

The cover is designed by Siddharth Suresh Thakur, to whom I am thankful as he worked on it after a simple request. The cover design displays the true nature of this story, and I am very grateful for his work on it.

Mr. Jairoop Jeevan and Deepaq Garg—my friends, philosophers and guides. Big thanks to both of them for constantly motivating and honing my skills. They are my true well-wishers.

I thank my father-in-law, Lt. Shri Kamal Kumar Jaiswal, for bestowing me with his blessings and trusting me.

To my family—Mr. Bishwanath Das (my father), Sonali Jaiswal, Kunal Jaiswal and Paulomi Jaiswal. Thanks to all of you for having faith in me.

Thanks to my loving daughter, Tushita, for her wonderfully innocent prayers for my success and happiness. She would often pray: "*Bhagwanji, mere Papa ka kaam jaldi se karva do,* please (Dear Lord, please get my father's work done soon)." I hope, my little angel, your prayers will be heard by God one day.

I am grateful to the team at Wordit Content Design and Editing Services, Mumbai. Thank you to Linta Antony for introducing me to Malini Nair, who patiently heard my manuscript and provided me with the best team ever.

I thank Yash Vadalia and Niyati Joshi for ensuring that my work was handled well. Thanks to Rinky Gopalani, the Project Head, for the timely execution and completion of the task at hand, and last but not the least, I sincerely thank Shruti Bhiwandiwala, for her extensive editing skills that have changed the face of my story and transformed it into an enthralling read. It was a great honour to work with her; I had an unforgettable experience, and I wish her luck and hope to work with her in the future as well.

Finally, thanks to everyone else involved with this book in one way or the other. If I have missed out on thanking you personally, know that there will be more books in the future for that.

About the Author

Parthasarthi Daas was born in Bhusawal, Maharashtra, on 7th March, 1973 and was raised in Kolkata and Indore during his early years. He has a Master of Philosophy degree with a specialisation in German Science and Vedic Astrology. He has an acute interest in copywriting, and has scripted many TV commercials.

He was a columnist for the Times of India, Navbharat Times, and Dainik Bhaskar. He has worked with Rajkumar Santoshi (eminent filmmaker) and Maqbool Fida Husain as an assistant director for their feature films, and has also held the post of Executive Producer at Zee TV. He has designed and headed two courses for Whistling Woods International, Mumbai.

Daas currently resides in Mumbai with his wife and five-year-old daughter. He believes in simple living and high thinking, and hopes to become a renowned author and revolutionary filmmaker some day.

For feedback email: parthsarrthi@gmail.com